Joaquin was sitting ramrod straight in the front seat.

Lali wanted to ask what had happened, but he didn't seem open to questions.

As if reading her mind, Joaquin twisted around and looked at her son, who was entangled with his dog.

"Since you're going to the Tres Amigos ranch, you should keep Luna with you. You can drop her off at my place when you return to the cabin."

"You're not going?" That shouldn't upset her so much.

"Did I do something wrong?" Oscar spoke for the first time.

"It's me. I have..." Joaquin paused, turned away from them and looked out the window. "I just need to figure some stuff out. It's better if I do it alone."

Wrapping her arms tighter around her middle, she suppressed the urge to reach out to him.

Her instinct was to soothe him, but she was in no place to help someone else. Her life was a mess, and she needed to focus on her son.

A seventh-generation Texan, **Jolene Navarro** fills her life with family, faith and life's beautiful messiness. She knows that as much as the world changes, people stay the same: vow-keepers and heartbreakers. Jolene married a vow-keeper who shows her holding hands never gets old. When not writing, Jolene teaches art to teens and hangs out with her own four almost-grown kids. Find Jolene on Facebook or her blog, jolenenavarro.com.

Books by Jolene Navarro

Love Inspired

The Ranchers of Rio Bella

The Texan's Unexpected Home
The Rancher's Christmas Gift

Lone Star Heritage

Bound by a Secret
The Reluctant Rancher
The Texan's Journey Home

Cowboys of Diamondback Ranch

The Texan's Secret Daughter
The Texan's Surprise Return
The Texan's Promise
The Texan's Unexpected Holiday
The Texan's Truth
Her Holiday Secret
Claiming Her Texas Family

Love Inspired Historical

Lone Star Bride

Visit the Author Profile page at LoveInspired.com for more titles.

THE RANCHER'S CHRISTMAS GIFT

JOLENE NAVARRO

LOVE INSPIRED
INSPIRATIONAL ROMANCE

If you purchased this book without a cover you should be aware that this book is stolen property. It was reported as "unsold and destroyed" to the publisher, and neither the author nor the publisher has received any payment for this "stripped book."

LOVE INSPIRED®
INSPIRATIONAL ROMANCE

ISBN-13: 978-1-335-23027-0

The Rancher's Christmas Gift

Copyright © 2025 by Jolene Navarro

All rights reserved. No part of this book may be used or reproduced in any manner whatsoever without written permission.

Without limiting the author's and publisher's exclusive rights, any unauthorized use of this publication to train generative artificial intelligence (AI) technologies is expressly prohibited.

This is a work of fiction. Names, characters, places and incidents are either the product of the author's imagination or are used fictitiously. Any resemblance to actual persons, living or dead, businesses, companies, events or locales is entirely coincidental.

For questions and comments about the quality of this book, please contact us at CustomerService@Harlequin.com.

® is a trademark of Harlequin Enterprises ULC.

Love Inspired
22 Adelaide St. West, 41st Floor
Toronto, Ontario M5H 4E3, Canada
www.LoveInspired.com

HarperCollins Publishers
Macken House, 39/40 Mayor Street Upper,
Dublin 1, D01 C9W8, Ireland
www.HarperCollins.com

Printed in U.S.A.

Recycling programs for this product may not exist in your area.

And there were in the same country shepherds abiding
in the field, keeping watch over their flock by night.
—*Luke* 2:8

This is dedicated to the memory of a cowboy who left us too soon, Douglas Brice. A true Texas cowboy with a heart of gold. And to his mother, Linda Kirkpatrick. Thank you for diligently preserving Texas Hill Country history in words and deeds.

Chapter One

Joaquin DeLeon leaned back in the chair, balancing on the back two legs. He really should get a rocker, but that made him feel even older than his forty-five years. The sky was clear tonight and there wasn't a moon to give any light.

But the stars were endless, like crushed diamonds scattered over a swath of dark purple velvet. He strummed a few chords on his old guitar, then winced when he hit the wrong note. Shadow and Luna, the two Akitas hanging out on the porch with him, didn't judge.

Training service companion dogs for wounded veterans gave him purpose that had eluded him. Shadow, his companion dog, had changed his life. His panic attacks and blackouts were gone. He was now giving that gift to other veterans. Training the rescued dogs fit perfectly into his life. Luna was his tenth dog, but she wasn't responding the way he'd expected.

He was letting the poor dog down. It wasn't her fault. She was smart, but he would have to call

Valerie at Paws for Soldiers and let her know it didn't seem to be working out.

Joaquin hated failure of any kind. He glanced at the gold-and-white Akita. What would happen to her if it didn't work out? She had already been dismissed from the military. He'd give it one more month before returning her to Valerie. But if they couldn't match her with a veteran, what would happen to her? Maybe he'd keep her as a pet. But if he joined the ranchers in the mountain of Matamoros, Mexico, it wouldn't be feasible.

With a heavy sigh, he tried a new chord. It was flat.

He should go to bed, but then he'd just toss and turn, unable to sleep. With a sigh, he started the song over. After serving in the army for twenty-two years he should be happy to be home. Secluded on the ranch, working with his specialized herd of cattle and horses, the life he'd built here should be enough. He was even restoring the pasturelands to native grasses. His family was just down the hill if they needed him.

But he was restless. Things were changing whether he liked it or not. He'd been working with the ranchers in the mountains of Mexico to build his herd of longhorns and mustangs. Now they were suggesting a more permanent role. In Mexico. And his baby sister was about to be married. He shifted in his chair. He was good with it. He really was.

He glanced at the dogs. "I had my doubts, but Kingston is good for my baby sister and her son." Happy endings didn't happen in their family. He prayed his sister would prove that theory wrong. She had to. But watching them together brought up too many...memories.

The past couldn't be changed so why think about it? It was the future now that was difficult to imagine.

Jupiter was bright tonight. "God, is there something I'm missing?" He opened his heart and listened. There was a verse about not being anxious but being grateful. Maybe in Philippians?

He should get his Bible, find the verse and pin it all over his cabin. Both dogs lifted their heads, then looked at him waiting for his reaction.

He laid his hand flat over the strings and listened. "What is it?"

In unison they looked back into the darkness. Headlights shone at the base of the hill. "Could be Isaac. Saw him leave about an hour ago." His youngest brother was the rookie veterinarian in town, so he got most of the middle-of-the-night emergencies.

The dogs weren't buying it. They stayed on alert.

The car didn't turn to the right—it was coming up the hill. He straightened. The headlights were unfamiliar. Not a family vehicle.

Sliding the guitar behind him, he estimated the time of arrival. Should he go inside the cabin where he could better protect himself and the dogs if needed? Paranoia might be making him overreact but it was better to be prepared than surprised.

Standing, he motioned for the dogs to follow him. Once inside he gave the silent command to sit. He waited at the door. With high beams on, the large vehicle pulled up to his steps and stopped. The night went silent when the engine was cut. Then the headlights went out. That wasn't smart on their part, because he could see clearly now. It was an old Range Rover. One that had clearly seen off-road action.

His blood pressure increased. The driver's door opened and so did the passenger's. It was impossible to keep his full attention on two targets. What threat was approaching? Shadow nudged his hand. His service dog knew when he was slipping out of reality. "Good boy."

Taking a deep breath, he anchored himself by burying his fingers in his dog's fur and touching the window frame on his door with his other hand. This was his cabin on the family ranch, not a dangerous assignment overseas.

He narrowed his gaze as a woman got out. That was a lot of white. Like a huge wedding dress.

What? The other passenger was a child, in a mini tuxedo and staring at a large digital pad. The blue light reflected off the boy's face as he gripped the device with both hands. He looked about the size of his sister's son, Leo, who was six.

Had he fallen asleep to find himself in a bizarre dream? He half expected an alien head to pop out of the wedding dress. He'd had that nightmare more than once.

The two retired military dogs stared at him, waiting for a command. Luna stayed against the wall. Shadow was at his side.

The woman lifted the bottom of her dress with one hand and marched up to his porch with confidence. Three bold knocks. The boy followed her, never taking his gaze off the screen. Luna and Shadow shifted, ready to spring, but were too well trained to make a sound or move without permission.

For once in his adult life, he didn't know what to do.

"Hello! Isaac?" Her voice had a slight accent, and was soft and very nonthreatening.

His shoulders fell with the release of tension. She was friends with his youngest brother. That explained a lot—still weird, but she was lost and looking for Isaac. He frowned. Who was she? His baby brother didn't have many friends outside of the family.

With one motion he reassured the dogs, but they stayed alert. He eased the door open.

She stepped back, eyes wide, pushing her son behind her and out of his sight.

Joaquin knew what she saw. There was nothing friendly or welcoming about him. Untrimmed hair and beard. He was six-four to her five-three, maybe, and he was two hundred thirty pounds of ex-military strength. It was hard to estimate any other details under all that fabric. Unless she had a hidden weapon, she wasn't a threat.

"You're not Isaac. Where is he?" Her voice was sharp. She glared at him as if he had messed up her whole night. Okay, so she wasn't scared of him like most people.

"Not here." He relaxed, leaned his shoulder against the door frame and crossed his arms. This was getting interesting.

After a moment of her glaring, he almost grinned at the way she managed to look down her nose at him. "Who are you?" she asked.

"The better question is who are you?" He glanced at the dress and back to her face.

She blinked, then looked down like she had forgotten the whole white silk thing, but she didn't say a word.

"Should I be worried for my baby brother? You're the one knocking on my door in the middle of the night in a wedding dress looking for Isaac."

She closed her eyes briefly. When she looked back up, there was a flash of desperation and something else he couldn't quite identify. His insides churned. He might have recognized it, but it would be easier to turn her away if he didn't put a name to the emotion.

"I'm Dr. Kan."

That he was not expecting. "You're Isaac's friend? The expert on caves?" He had pictured an old professor with white hair and pale skin due to the lack of sun. Could this night get any stranger?

He looked behind her at the little boy. "I assume he's not the groom?"

"No." She was back to being all business. The stone-cold face and the melodramatic wedding attire didn't match.

He raised an eyebrow waiting for an explanation.

She sighed, as if educating him was a true chore. "I was about to be married but the wedding was called off. It was a last-minute thing. I needed a place to go, far away from—" she waved a hand in the air "—there. I called Isaac about five hours ago and asked if I could come immediately. He said yes, but in the last twenty minutes I haven't been able to reach him. I followed the directions to the ranch. He said his apartment was past the main house. Obviously, I made a wrong turn." She paused to catch her breath. Then surveyed the area with concern. "Am I on his ranch?"

He gave her a nod.

After a minute of silence, she started talking again. "It has been an unusually tense day. When Isaac called and told me about the cave you'd found I wasn't available to examine it. But the idea of an unknown cave that hasn't had human interference is a gold mine of Earth's ancient history. I've never been the first scientist in any cave." She took another breath. "Sorry, my mind is usually much more focused than this and stays on one path at a time. Right now, I would like to find Isaac and secure a quiet place to change and sleep." She waved behind her. "My son, Oscar, is with me."

"Let's start over. Hola. I'm Joaquin DeLeon of Rio Bella, Texas. One of Isaac's older brothers."

The corner of her lips curled, not in a smiling way but more of a you-are-a-boy-in-a-man's-body sort of way. She held out her hand and sighed. "Hola. Dr. Xitlali Kan. Professor of Environmental Engineering, Quantitative Paleobiology and incompleteness of geological records. Basically, anything to do with ancient Earth history."

He stood straighter. "Xitlali? That's Aztec. Do

you spell it with the original *X* or has it been changed to the *C*?"

Surprise widened her eyes, then her expression softened. "My father is very proud of his Aztec bloodlines and uses the authentic spelling of Nahuatl. That's one of several languages he speaks. So, it is the *X*, but I do use the *C* when someone is announcing me, so they pronounce it right. But when I'm in the States I go by Lali. It's just easier. Do you speak Nahuatl?"

A soft chime came from the tablet. The boy moved next to his mother and handed her the device. "It's 2300 hours." He promptly removed his jacket, then sat to take off his shoes.

"He knows military time?" That was surprising. Joaquin could identify with getting out of formal clothes as soon as possible.

Ignoring him, she bent down to try to stop her son. "Oscar, no. Not here." Her voice was low and calm, but there was an edge of desperation to it.

"Abuela said we can take off our special wedding clothes at 2300 hours, not a minute earlier," the boy said as if reciting someone's orders. He took off his sock, wiggled his toes and giggled.

Joaquin grinned. The night continued to surprise him. This was the most fun he'd had in a long time.

"Oscar." The one word was low and through

gritted teeth. Holding her right hand like an axe she slammed it down to her open palm.

She had quit talking and was telling him to stop in sign language.

"No. I want them off now." He was getting upset as he pulled at the other shoe, and she tried to stop him. Then he yanked on his bow tie.

Joaquin lowered himself to become smaller. Was there something he could do to help? He didn't want to make the situation worse. The boy's reaction reminded him of Isaac when he was younger. His brother used to throw a fit when something set him off and he'd become hyperfocused on that one thing.

These two had obviously had a rough day. Luna, the three-year-old Akita, looked up at him and whined.

The mom in the wedding dress stayed silent but used hand signals. At this point any sound would probably overstimulate the boy. Joaquin's family hadn't understood that when Isaac was younger.

"Is he scared of dogs?" Joaquin kept his voice low as he directed it to Dr. Kan.

She turned and looked at him as if she had forgotten he was there. That stung the pride a bit.

"What?" She glanced at Luna.

"Luna's in training to be a service dog for veterans with PTSD. She's asking permission to approach."

"He likes dogs." With a nod she agreed, and Joaquin gave Luna permission.

The white-and gold Akita stayed low as she nosed the boy. Oscar stilled and opened his eyes. Luna laid her big head on his leg. He dug a hand into her thick fur and his sobs receded.

This was a good sign. Maybe there was hope for Luna. She had been released from the army because children in distress distracted her from her job of sniffing out bombs and weapons.

He understood all too well how children could derail focus from one's duty.

Lali refused to give in to the tears that burned her eyes. Wanting to avoid one of Oscar's massive meltdowns was the only reason she had stayed in the ridiculous wedding dress for hours. Matias had slipped into her dressing room to tell her he couldn't go through with the wedding just minutes before the ceremony. He'd said it was too much pressure for him.

For him? They'd both been startled when she'd laughed out loud. Not the response he'd expected. Maybe this was the moment she was meant to start doing the unexpected. To avoid a discussion with her parents about this perfect marriage they wanted, she'd taken her son's hand and left through the back door. Then, sitting behind her steering wheel trying to explain the change of plans to Oscar, she'd realized she had nowhere to go.

All of her family and friends had been inside the church waiting for her to walk down the aisle.

Except for Isaac. He never went to events with groups of strange people. She hadn't seen him since their days at College Station. But he had reached out to her a few weeks ago about a job. His family had found a cave on their ranch, and he'd asked if she could survey it. She'd been excited. Unexpected manna for her research, but she had told him she probably couldn't do it due to other obligations. Like her wedding.

She was free now and a Texas Hill Country ranch with a newly found cave sounded like the best Christmas gift ever. She needed a safe place to recover, ponder her new life choices and rest. So, she'd called Isaac, a friend her parents didn't know anything about.

Oscar was fixated on the tablet her mother had given him. Esmeralda Puentes-Kan had given strict orders that no one was to take off a stitch of wedding outfits until the time she had set. Continuity was important for the pictures.

Lali blew out a puff of air but none of the frustration escaped with it. She had hoped to be inside when the timer went off.

Afraid of the judgment she would see in the stranger's eyes, she had avoided him to the point of being rude. Gritting her back teeth, she finally looked up. What she observed was startling. His grayish-green eyes were full of compassion, *not* condescension.

She steadied her breathing. "I apologize for intruding on your evening. The arrangements were made at the last minute, but Isaac said we could come tonight. We've been in the car for over five hours. Do you know where he is?"

The man watched the interaction between his dog and Oscar with the intensity she used when analyzing new discoveries. She was talking to herself.

Oscar hadn't really understood the wedding ceremony and he had never clicked with Matias, so the lack of a ceremony hadn't upset him. But her mother had drilled into his brain they had to wear these clothes until 11:00 p.m.

She hadn't had the energy to deal with a meltdown. Oscar was very good at following clear expectations. Flexibility from a hardwired rule was not in his toolbox, so they had left the Woodlands with wedding clothes on. Now she stood on a stranger's porch in layers of ivory silk and her son was not at his best. She was surprised Isaac's brother hadn't closed his door and locked it.

The man's stature was imposing. She was very aware of him and didn't like it.

Oscar laid his head on the dog's neck. This

was a record for deescalating a meltdown. She reached over and gently removed his bow tie, helped him slip the dress shirt off, leaving him in his favorite T-shirt. She took a deep breath. Crisis averted.

With the now-crushed silk tie in her hand she stood. "Like I said, we've been in the car for a long time. If you can just point me in the direction of Isaac's place, we'll get out of your way."

The mountain of a man stood and shook his head. His dark wavy hair fell over his forehead. It looked as if he hadn't had it cut in a while.

"Isaac left a little over an hour ago. Probably on an emergency call. No telling when he'll be back. If you know Isaac, you know how focused he is on a project. I doubt he's going to check his phone anytime soon. There's a good possibility he forgot you were coming." He rubbed the back of his neck, then looked over her shoulder.

"His place is an efficiency over his equine center. You don't want to wait there. There's one empty room in the main house, but we'd have to wake everyone up." He scanned the darkness as if looking for solutions.

"We don't need much." She heard the pathetic pleading in her voice but couldn't find enough energy to care. "I can wait at Isaac's. I just can't spend any more time in this dress."

He frowned. "Of course not. Not far from here

is the hunter's lodge. It should be good. It's a little farther up the hill. No one goes up there without passing my place. It has two bedrooms and a loft. If you don't like it, we can find you somewhere else tomorrow."

"Sounds perfect." Tension she hadn't even been aware of left her shoulders. Even if it was an old hunter's lodge, it was better than any of her other options, which were none. "Thank you."

"Let me get my keys."

Oscar started rocking and humming. It was way past his bedtime. How had she gotten them into this mess? She lowered her head and massaged her temples. Because she hadn't followed her heart and was afraid of her parents. The one time she'd strayed off the path they had laid out for her had been disastrous.

Closing her eyes, she took a deep breath. She had really liked Matias. They were good lab partners and had much in common with their research goals. That was it. Her parents adored him. But calling it off was the right thing to do. She should have been brave enough to end it weeks ago.

The door opened. Joaquin lifted his free hand and, with his fingers making an *R*, shook it back and forth. He was looking at Oscar. He had asked if he was ready to go.

Her son nodded and stood.

"You know ASL?"

"I noticed you were using it with him. Is it okay?" He frowned.

"He was nonverbal until a little over a year ago. I had started signing simple words when he was a toddler, but our vocabulary grew as he got older and didn't start talking."

Her parents refused to use sign language. They insisted it was the reason he wasn't speaking and accused her of babying him to the point of stunting his development.

The word *lazy* had been tossed around. Anger she'd kept bottled up pushed at the now-fragile restraints. Her parents hadn't wanted to see the truth, so she'd tried to placate them.

She was done. Everything she did from here on out was for her son. "Now he'll sometimes go into a hyperverbal mode for a stretch of time." But never in front of her parents. She wasn't sure if it was a blessing or not.

With a nod, Joaquin accepted it without question and went to the huge black truck parked on the side of his cabin. He opened the back door and motioned for the dogs to get in. The one that had stayed by his side jumped in, his tail wagging. He seemed excited about the unexpected trip.

Luna hung back and licked Oscar's hand before leaping into the back seat.

"It's not far," Joaquin said as he got in and closed the driver's side door.

She sighed. Right now, everything seemed out of reach. Like a home where she could raise her son with a family who valued him. A place to do her research where she could dream of ways to make a better world.

A man who would understand all that and not just want her to improve his life. Avery, her first husband and Oscar's dad, had wanted her to take care of the messiness of life, and Matias wanted her to better his career.

She and Oscar got in their Rover and followed Joaquin's taillights. *Okay, God. I get it. I'm grateful for my son and my research. At least I can focus on those.*

Two out of three wasn't bad.

Chapter Two

Lali put her Rover in Park and looked up at the two-story log cabin. With its deep porch and huge balcony, it was straight out of a vacation brochure. Floor-to-ceiling windows covered the front, and the back disappeared into the rocky hillside. It looked more like a setting in Colorado than Texas.

He hadn't exaggerated. It didn't take them long to get to the lodge. They could have walked. But it was dark.

She helped Oscar out of the Rover. Instead of his tablet he hugged his pillow. That was a good sign.

Not a single light came from the building or around it. When she looked up, the stars were awe-inspiring. With no light pollution, the sky was majestic and vast, making her problems seem small. She pointed it out to Oscar.

He gasped. "It's like the poem I wrote."

Joaquin and the dogs joined them. "You can't

get that view in the city. Do you remember your poem?" he asked.

Oscar nodded but didn't take his gaze from the night sky. "'In the stars, a wondrous tale unfolds, where celestial bodies dance and life takes hold. God's solar system, a family so grand, Luna the matriarch so radiant stands. Planets like children orbit with grace; what makes each unique is embraced. Inner planets, rocky and bold, Venus, Earth and Mars, stories yet untold.'"

She casually wiped her face, hoping they wouldn't notice her tears. It was so silly to cry, but why couldn't her parents see how special their grandson was?

"That's beautiful, Oscar." She adjusted her backpack to keep herself from hugging him close.

As usual, Oscar didn't respond, just kept staring at the sky as if documenting each star.

She glanced at Joaquin, interested in seeing his reaction, then bit back a smile. His jaw was hanging open. "Well." His gaze met hers. "So that's what hyperverbal means. That was something." He looked at her son. "How old are you?"

She liked the way he talked directly to Oscar. But instead of answering, he crossed his arms and looked down. She answered out of habit. "He's eight. Almost nine."

"Oh. I thought he was younger." Then he

looked as if he regretted the words. "I mean not that—"

"He's small for his age." Also, most people didn't expect an eight-year-old to throw the kind of fit he had on the porch.

"Well, Oscar," Joaquin said, looking up. "I'm pretty sure all I could ever manage is 'Roses are red.'"

Oscar lifted his chin and finished Joaquin's line. "Moon is sometimes blue. But the stars can never shine as bright as you. My mom's name means *star* in Nahuatl."

With a deep laugh, Joaquin shook his head. "See, even in that, you outdo me. You're brilliant." He signed the last word. Then he went up the steps to the cabin.

This man seemed unreal. He casually accepted Oscar as he was. A strange woman in a wedding dress showed up at his door in the middle of the night, and he just went along with it, making sure they had a safe place to sleep.

She should have left the academic world long ago if this was the norm for mountain men.

But then again, she wasn't in a good mental state. In the clear light of day, he might not appear as charming. She had just been left at the altar—metaphorically speaking, since she hadn't even made it down the aisle.

She picked up the hem of her dress to make it

up the steps. Was it metaphorical if she was in a wedding dress? Her brain needed sleep. And something to focus on. Like the cave. This was a true blessing.

An outside light came on. A porch swing, four rocking chairs and small vintage tables scattered around the area invited people to gather. The front door was heavily carved wood and stained glass.

"This is a hunting lodge?" She had expected something much more primitive.

"My oldest brother builds things when he's stressed. He built it for his wife while she was going through cancer treatment. It was basically a one-room shed with a bathroom before he started."

He opened the door without knocking.

"They're not here?" She didn't want to intrude on someone else's space. She glanced at her phone to see if Isaac had returned her texts. He had rarely talked about his family, or about anything other than whatever they had been studying at the time.

"Cyrus and his daughter have lived in the main house for a while now. It doesn't get used as much as it should."

He turned on the lights, showcasing a large rock fireplace surrounded by an inviting sitting arrangement of two sofas and stuffed chairs. It was mainly neutrals with accents of deep reds and some yellow. Fuzzy blankets and throw pillows were everywhere.

Opposite was an open kitchen with a redbrick wall. A table for eight separated the two spaces. The front windows behind her were two stories tall and the loft was over the kitchen. Three closed doors led off the main area.

Her mouth fell open when she turned and saw the large reading nook between the front windows and stairs. The back wall was floor-to-ceiling books. She itched to explore the titles. There was a thin layer of dust, but not as bad as she'd expected.

Oscar walked in behind her hugging his pillow.

"My sister comes up once a week to make sure it's clean. Emma, my niece, has had some sleepovers up here and we've rented it out a few times. It's all yours tonight and for as long as you need it."

He went to a narrow door behind the stairs and pulled out sheets. The fact that he didn't mention the wife and mother wasn't good and she didn't want to ask.

She followed him into a bedroom off the kitchen. He was making a king-size bed. "There are blankets and pillows in the cedar chest."

"It's beautiful. The whole place is stunning. But is it weird that it also feels loved? It's like it was waiting for us." She should not have said that out loud. She had never had a dream house; now she did and this was it.

He smiled. "Charlene loved going on weekend trips just to hunt down the perfect piece for each spot." He tucked the last sheet corner under the bed and stood. His gaze lingered over each picture and piece of furniture. His jaw flexed and there was a long silence. Was he reliving his memories of his sister-in-law? Was he going to get emotional?

Emotions were not rational and therefore dangerous. Being an intruder into someone else's emotional memories was not comfortable. She glanced at her phone. Where was Isaac? She needed to get away from the mountain man as quickly as possible.

Joaquin hadn't been to Cyrus and Charlene's house since the funeral, seven years ago. Avoiding places that triggered heavy emotions was the best way to remain steady and calm. But bringing Dr. Kan and her son here had felt right. Didn't mean he wanted to talk about it.

He finally looked at her. She was chewing on her bottom lip and staring at her phone as if it were a lifeline. His lack of social skills was showing.

"Sorry. I was thinking about what you said.

Charlene would be happy you and your son have the cabin to stay in. She wanted it to be a retreat from the world."

Looking much more relaxed, Lali picked up a blanket and spread it over the bed. "Thank you for bringing us here. I need to get a few things from the car. Oscar brought his pillow in with him. He'll stay in here with me." Her eyes went wide. "Oh, Oscar." She darted to the door. "I've been so enthralled by the house I lost track of my son."

"He's in the living room with the dogs." But she was already gone before he could finish.

Coming up next to her, he smiled. She stood with one hand over her mouth and the other over her chest. Shadow stood guard at the door. On the short sofa, Oscar was curled up around his pillow with one of Charlene's favorite blankets. Luna was sitting on the floor but had her muzzle on the boy's arm, watching him as he slept. Oscar's other hand rested in her fur.

"Luna's not allowed on furniture. But she looks as if she is contemplating breaking that rule to get closer to him." At the sound of her name, the dog's eyes darted to him, but she didn't move.

"He never falls asleep easily in strange places." The white skirt of her dress billowed around her as she sat in the chair next to her son. "He's so tired. I'll sleep on the other sofa so when he wakes up, I'm here."

Joaquin eased down in the chair he always sat in the few times he had visited Cyrus and Charlene. "Why don't you go get your bag? I'll watch over him."

She sighed. "Good idea. Thank you." She went back out the front door.

With a two-finger motion he called Shadow to him. The dog happily took a few pats, then lay down at his feet. Peace washed over Joaquin. He had forgotten how comforting the lodge was.

This was the strangest night. Never in a million years could he have anticipated a runaway bride on his doorstep.

Wait. Did she call it off or had she been jilted? She'd never said. He couldn't imagine anyone leaving her at the altar.

He had the uneasy feeling she could completely disrupt his world. Her visit should be brief.

She should be going home for Christmas. How long did it take to survey a cave? There was also the college where she worked. Isaac might have told Joaquin which one, but truthfully, he hadn't cared where the professor came from. He didn't like the idea of strangers on his land poking around that cave. In spite of it, he smiled. He might have made more of an effort if he had known... *Nope, not going there.*

It didn't matter. Starting tomorrow Dr. Kan and her son were Isaac's problem. And Abigail's, probably. Hospitality was in his sister's blood, and she was on the team that wanted to open the cave to the public.

If Joaquin had his way, they would cover it up and pretend it wasn't there. His grandfather was right. The more people that knew about it the more trespassers would be on their land.

It had already started.

Chapter Three

Warm sunshine tickled her eyelids, which were sealed shut. It took some effort, but she finally got them open. Lali blinked, not recognizing the room. Sitting up, she looked for Oscar. He was spread eagle at the bottom of the bed, stress free. He had kicked off the covers and was still in his dress slacks, but his feet and chest were bare. Then her wedding day rushed into her sleep-fogged mind.

She wasn't married. Her heart thumped hard against her chest. For the last year her future had been tied to Matias. Doubt and uncertainty had been her silent burden the whole time. Now the light weight of relief floated through her. An unknown future was better than the path her parents had laid out for her and Oscar.

A messy pile of white covered a chair in the corner of the room. It was no longer her wedding dress. A smile slowly pulled at her lips. She would take a few days to readjust her thoughts and consider all her new possibilities. The best part was the opportunity to walk under the Earth in a space that hadn't been altered by human interference.

It was the perfect way to not deal with the mess of her personal life. Taking the dress to the closet, she hung it up. Looking down at her feet, she wiggled her toes. She loved the comfy joggers and fuzzy socks that were her go-to stressed outfit. Her parents hated this outfit. They said even alone one should dress with poise and dignity.

Her parents. She still had to talk to them. Soon, but not now. It was the morning after her non–wedding day. She needed to readjust. It was a big pivot.

She couldn't shake the feeling deep in her gut that today was a new start. She had pushed herself out of the cocoon and now it was time to test her wings. Was she strong enough to fly?

Her phone was face down. It could stay that way for now. Without a doubt there would be calls and texts waiting for her.

What had Matias told them? She'd left him to handle her parents on his own. Had he admitted to them he had called it off, or with her gone had he used her as a scapegoat? Last night she'd sent a text just telling them she was fine but then ignored all notifications.

What she was, was a coward. No, she was taking time to heal and find a new path.

A knock on the front door pulled her out of her musings. Oscar sat up and rubbed his eyes. He looked around and pulled his pillow against his chest. Waking up in a strange place usually didn't go well with him, but he seemed very calm.

In a rush, she picked up his backpack and gave it to him. "Good morning, sweetheart. We spent the night in a cabin on my friend's ranch. Remember how I told you about Isaac? The one with the new cave."

He nodded. "Where's Luna?"

"They went home after you fell asleep on the couch."

Joaquin had carried her son to bed so she wouldn't have to wake him up. He'd left quickly after that. Not that she had wanted him to hang around and talk, but it was a little disappointing the way he rushed out.

The knock sounded again. "That's probably Isaac. Change your clothes and brush your teeth. The bathroom is in there." The barn door hung on the wall looked very authentic.

She couldn't wait to get into that incredible shower. Whoever designed it had soothing comfort in mind.

Her son gathered his backpack and pushed the door to the side. She ran her fingers through her hair and went into the living room.

It wasn't Isaac. Joaquin DeLeon stood outside

her door. But he had turned and was now going down the steps.

"Hey. Sorry I was late getting to the door. Had to make sure Oscar was good." The porch faced the southeast. The sun was coming up over the hills, caressing the valley with warm, early-morning light. Stepping out, she was stunned by the view. "I can see the river. It's so clear. Is that your ranch?"

"Some of it is. It used to all be part of a Spanish land grant. Over the generations most of it was lost. But we still have enough to manage. The opening to the cave is south of here." He pointed behind them.

"I can't tell you how excited I am to see it."

He grunted.

"You're not excited?"

"I'd rather not have strangers traipsing around our property. Isaac said we could trust you, but..." He shrugged as if he hadn't just insulted her.

"Oh." Feeling awkward, she studied the landscape. "Look. There's a whole herd of longhorns. I've only ever seen one or two at a time. Are they yours?"

He moved closer and they stood shoulder to shoulder. Kind of—he was a foot taller than her. There was pride in his single nod. "I've put them together from wild herds in the mountains of Mexico. Using DNA I've reconstructed a herd of the original cattle that started our vaquero history. With help from Isaac, of course."

"Really?" *Why would he say of course?* She lifted her gaze to his. "That's fascinating. How did you—"

His head tilted and his eyes narrowed. The intensity was back in his—last night they looked grayish green, but now in the morning light they looked violet. Whatever color they were, they were focused on her cheek.

Time warped and slowed down as she watched his hand move closer to her face. He was going to touch her. She almost leaned in but coming to her senses stepped away quickly. At the opposite corner of the porch, she crossed her arms.

"Sorry. That was rude." He pointed to his face. "You have something on your upper cheek. Is it a squashed spider or…?" He wiggled his finger over his left eye. "And your other eye."

In horror she wiped her face. Sure enough, it was her false eyelash. No wonder it was so hard to open her eyes this morning. The other one was still partially attached. She pulled it off.

"Ouch." There was probably a better way to do that, and it should have been done last night. She just wasn't used to having things on her face that had to be properly removed.

"Is Luna here?" Oscar ran out the door. He signed, *Moon*.

With a sigh of relief, she checked her face and hair as Joaquin's focus turned to her son.

"She is." He made a motion and Luna bounded up the steps and went right to her son.

Oscar hugged the dog.

"He speaks Spanish too?" Joaquin looked at her.

Her face had to be red. She kept her gaze fixed on her son. The man just a few feet away was too much to look at. "I think so. I've noticed he'll translate between languages with signs. My parents speak Spanish, Nahuatl, German and English. He has words in all of them, when he wants to use them. I can't tell if he knows they're separate languages."

"Interesting." He knelt on the other side of the dog, giving her son space. It put him much closer to her again.

"Luna wanted to come and make sure that everything in the cabin worked for you. Did you sleep well?"

Her son nodded.

"Good." He lifted a bag she hadn't noticed earlier. "And she was worried you'd be hungry."

"Thank you. We just woke up, so food has not been an issue yet." Why was she still standing here? "Come in."

"I'm sorry. I didn't mean to wake you up." He followed her in, went to the narrow island and pulled items out of his bag. "You had a long day, but I was… Well, I mean I didn't want Oscar to go hungry on his first day on the ranch."

Her throat burned. This stranger cared more about her son's mental state than anyone else in their life. Was it because of his brother? He understood her son wasn't throwing a fit because he was a brat that lacked discipline, but that as a neurodivergent child he had different needs.

Oscar sat on one of the overstuffed chairs so he could watch what Joaquin was doing. His attention was split between the dog and the man. He was also trying to convince Luna to sit next to him on the chair. She had her head rested on his leg and made a sound that was somewhere between a whine and bark.

Joaquin stopped what he was doing and went over to them. "I don't allow the dogs on the furniture, but if it's okay with your mom, I'll let Luna follow your command."

She nodded without hesitation. Her son had never bonded to anyone so fast.

Balancing on his haunches, Joaquin lowered himself to be eye level with Oscar. "She reads signs, so point your index finger to the ceiling once and she'll know she can get up on the chair. If you do it twice, she'll go up the stairs. So be careful." Joaquin did the motion and Oscar copied him.

There was literal joy on the dog's face. In one motion she was on the chair. She settled close to Oscar and sighed as if she had been waiting forever to be next to him.

Joaquin laughed. "Now that Luna's happy, let's talk about breakfast." He went back to the kitchen.

"Do you mind if I take a fast shower?" she asked.

"Take a long shower if you need to. We'll get breakfast done. Do you have anything you love or hate?"

She wanted to kiss him. *Nope*. That was not a rational thought. Where had it come from? A tired, overwhelmed brain. That's all it was. "I'm easy. Just no onions. Other than that, I'm game for anything."

"Got it. Anything I need to know about Oscar that he might not tell me?"

"As long as his food isn't touching or mushy he's fine."

She hesitated for a minute and watched Joaquin move around the kitchen. He washed his hands, then rinsed out a skillet. He paused and looked back at her. "Are you okay?"

Putting on a smile, she nodded. "I'm good. Just slow to move." She most absolutely without question was not okay. She had never seen any man so comfortable in the kitchen. To be honest, she had only been around three men in the kitchen, so her data weren't creditable.

Turning, she rushed back into the bedroom and stopped dead in her tracks when she saw her reflection.

She was a walking disaster area. No wonder Mr. Mountain Man looked at her weird. He could use a shave and trim, but she needed an all-day grooming session.

This was so embarrassing.

Joaquin let out a breath. What was wrong with him? He had been around beautiful, smart women before. He had reached out and almost touched her face without permission. Maybe he had taken the lone-wolf persona too far and needed to socialize more. It was an important part of the dogs' training.

Then again it might be best if he disengaged completely.

For now, he needed to get Dr. Kan and Oscar fed and turned over to Isaac, or better yet, Abigail. He shouldn't even be here, but last night he'd been unable to sleep. Was the cabin safe? Was there food? Was she emotionally distraught? He had been close to marriage once and it was hard shifting gears. She had shown up in her wedding dress. He blew out a puff of air. He didn't want to contemplate the heartache she must be going through.

His sister should be here. Abigail knew how to take care of people and their hurts. Talking was her thing. Isaac, on the other hand, was more clueless than Joaquin was.

Isaac would probably forget to feed himself if it wasn't for their sister. He most certainly would not make sure his guest who he'd invited had what they needed. He hadn't even made sure they'd had a safe place to sleep after telling them they could come. Joaquin loved his baby brother and was amazed at everything he had accomplished, but being social and taking care of people was not in his wheelhouse.

If Dr. Kan hadn't stumbled across his cabin last night... No, just deal with the facts. The here and now. They'd knocked on his door, and he'd brought them here and made sure they had breakfast. He couldn't let the spiral of doom start spinning.

"So, Oscar. First, I have bacon and sausage. Which do you want?"

Lifting his hand off Luna, he signed, *Both.*

"All right then."

Another grin and nod. Luna licked her lips like she knew she was getting some too. He'd have to make sure Oscar didn't overfeed her.

"Eggs?"

"Round," Oscar said.

"Round it is."

He slipped a tray of bacon in the oven and put the round sausage patties in the skillet. Then he dug through the gadget drawer and found the round silicone thingy that made perfectly round eggs. "My brother Isaac likes round food too. Leo, my nephew, loves animal-shaped food." He put toast in the toaster and flipped the sausage.

In the bottom cabinet, he looked for the box of Charlene's cookie cutters. Finding them, he spread them over the island. "We can make the toast any shape you want."

Oscar came over and sat on the stool across from him. His eyes went wide.

Joaquin pointed at the metal shapes. "Look. We have wild African animals, farm animals and several dinosaurs. Those are Leo's favorites."

On his knees, Oscar leaned over and touched a long-necked one.

With a smile, Joaquin picked it up and studied it. "Good choice."

The boy nodded. "Brontosaurus. Thunder Lizard."

"Brontosaurus toast it is." The toast popped up on cue. He buttered it and handed it to Oscar. "Do you want to do the cutting?"

They worked in silence as Joaquin finished

the rest of the food and Oscar cut the dinosaur toast. He pulled three plates out and rinsed them. "Orange juice?"

"Yes."

"Wow. I'm impressed." Lali came out of the room looking fresh and relaxed.

The OJ Joaquin was pouring almost flowed over the rim. Stopping in time, he picked it up and took a long sip as he righted his brain.

Her dark hair was damp hanging in relaxed waves barely touching her shoulders. He had never thought about bangs on a woman before, but they framed her face and made her large, dark eyes stand out. He had heard the expression of bow lips, and now he knew what it meant.

Forcing his gaze to go down to the eggs, he halted any thoughts he shouldn't have. He lifted the pan, sliding the round eggs onto the waiting plates. Then he carefully put two strips of bacon and two round sausages. "I have strawberries and bananas."

Oscar signed, *Yes*.

He handed Oscar a plastic knife and two bananas. "If you cut these, I'll cut the strawberries. Triangles or round?"

"Triangles," Oscar said very seriously.

"Fruit is his favorite." She went to her son's side. When she tried to push his hair down, he grunted and shifted away.

"Mom, I made Brontosaurus toast."

Acting like he didn't notice the rebuff and the hurt in her eyes, Joaquin put the plates and drinks in front of them and sat on the side. He wanted to warn Oscar that he might not always have his mom and to cherish every touch, but it wasn't his place.

"How did you get the eggs so round?" she asked as she forked her egg.

Oscar was carefully using a spoon to break off the edge of his egg without messing up the shape.

"Isaac likes round food too. When Charlene discovered that, she found this gadget that would cook anything that was liquidly into a circle. Eggs are the easiest. It was still here."

"Are you a secret Mr. Mom or Spec Ed teacher in disguise?" She sat and took off the head of her dinosaur with an exaggerated bite. Oscar giggled and did the same.

"Nope, just a cool uncle and remorseful brother." Isaac's childhood could have been so much better if they had taken the time to figure out what was really going on with him.

"Remorseful?" she said between bacon bites.

"We didn't understand what Isaac was going through his whole childhood and teen years. Everyone said it was grief. He lost both parents, his uncle and his grandmother who used to watch him when Mom went to work. They were just gone from our lives without warning. It was a car accident."

"I didn't know that. How old was he?"

"Four. Even before then he hadn't talked much. But then he'd have these huge, epic fits over what seemed like nothing. He would break things and scream. Then he would fall apart and cry for what seemed like hours. We had no clue what to do. Abigail, his twin, was the only one who could even get close to calming him when it happened. It was stressful on top of our own grief. I took the easy way out and left for the army."

Her brows went up. "The army was the easy way out?"

"I like problems I can fix." He didn't want to get into the emotional tornado they'd all been dealing with at the loss of their parents and grandmother. They had been the core that held the family together. He forced another bite of egg down.

She just watched him, waiting for more. Everyone else had stopped expecting more from him. She didn't know any better. He pushed the food around on his plate.

"When I would come home to visit, I didn't have any patience with him. I was very vocal about my belief that they were being too lenient." He closed his eyes and smothered the guilt. Oscar was having a silent conversation with his dino toast and Luna. "It's humbling to know how wrong I was. But as he got older the extreme fits went away, and he started acting..." He paused, searching for the right word. "What everyone considered normal. His teachers said he was bored because he was so much smarter than his classmates. They put him in smaller classes with a challenging curriculum. We thought he was better."

"He had taught himself to camouflage."

He nodded. "Everyone just said he was a quirky kid. Too smart for his own good. We couldn't keep up with him. When he came home from college telling us about neurodiversity and the spectrum, we were floored. At first my grandfather said it was hogwash, but Abigail did her research. I was overseas and did a deep dive into the topic." It was a God thing that Isaac turned out so well. "We made his childhood worse than it should have been. Now we make sure he has round pancakes and eggs."

Tears were threatening to spill over her eyelashes. "That's nice."

He looked away. "It's the right thing to do. We should have done it sooner."

Oscar slipped a piece of bacon to Luna. He should talk to Oscar later about feeding Luna table food. But then again, they weren't going to be around each other much.

She frowned and pushed her half-empty plate away. "My parents don't accept that their grandson is neurodivergent. They blame it on his father. And that I'm not strong enough with him. I've been accused of being too lenient. They were convinced he needed a strong father figure like Matias. I feel like I'm in the battle alone with no reinforcements."

Studying her son, she had a watery smile and looked to be on the edge of tears. Meanwhile the boy carefully took apart his egg.

The strong urge to protect her flooded his system. But it wasn't his job. No one had asked for his help. And they were getting way too personal. "Isaac said you would be discreet about the cave. With everything going on are you sure you're up for the task?"

Her spine stiffened and her jaw hardened. "Don't you concern yourself about me. Regardless of my personal life, I am recognized as one of the top professionals in this specialized field. And I agree at this point that the fewer who know about the cave the better."

He relaxed a bit. They were back to standing on nonemotional solid ground. "Do you need a couple of days to…?" He shrugged. What did one normally do the day or week after a wedding that didn't happen?

When his one and only serious relationship

had ended, he had hidden on the ranch and submerged himself with work. He hadn't talked to anyone but his longhorns and horses. He'd also had enough self-awareness to know that wasn't how most people dealt with emotional trauma.

"What I need is to figure out childcare so I can see this cave. Isaac didn't give me much information. The main questions are how large the chamber is and is there more than one? What will be the required climbing gear? Is there water? And what kind of equipment, beyond the standard? We need a small team. Who would be best?"

She pulled out a leather-covered notebook and started writing. He didn't think she was talking to him, but he disliked one of the words she threw out.

"There will be no team."

She lifted her head and looked straight at him. "Collection data on this scale can't be done by one person. I've always—"

"Nope, the agreement was you." He stood and pointed at her, then lowered himself when Oscar looked up, eyes wide. Shadow came to his side and nudged his hand. He took a deep breath and evened his tone. "Isaac said you would come and tell us the impact or historical whatever, then leave. Just you."

He knew this was going to happen. As soon as one outsider knew about the cave it would spread.

Closing her book, she folded her hands. "I haven't been in the cave, so I am unsure of the requirements. I was listing all the possibilities."

"A team is not and will never be a possibility. It's you or no one." He wasn't going to give in on this. "My grandfather and oldest brother back me, and they are the ones who make the final decision for the ranch."

"Can I see the cave today?" Any warmth or friendliness was gone.

So, she wasn't the one with a broken heart. How long had her poor groom stood at the altar waiting? He could sympathize with the guy. There wasn't much a man could do when he got his heart thrown back at him. Had he been close to Oscar?

That had been the hardest part for Joaquin, losing touch with Ethan. He took a breath and scratched Shadow's ear. They weren't Celeste and Ethan. He just needed to keep his distance.

She would be leaving soon, especially if she wasn't allowed to have her team come in and do the work. "Either me or Cyrus can take you. He'll be at the main house."

There was a knock on the door.

"Hello?" A sweet Texas drawl floated from the opening door. "Oh, there you are. Sorry I'm late. I just saw all the texts a little while ago. I tried calling." She stopped in the middle of the living room. "Oh."

It was his sister, Abigail, with a welcome basket and huge smile. "Joaquin?" Smile gone, confusion wrinkled her face. "What are you doing here?"

He hadn't done anything wrong, so why did he feel guilty?

Chapter Four

Lali put her fork down and turned to face the newcomer. "Hi. You must be the sister, Abigail."

"Yes." The tall woman came forward with the basket in one arm and an outstretched hand that took Lali's in a welcoming shake. She had the same Spanish-moss-colored eyes as Isaac and Joaquin. But hers didn't hide behind the cold steel she had seen in both brothers' eyes.

Energy swirled around Abigail as she moved to the opposite side of the kitchen and placed her basket on the counter. "Sorry I didn't see the texts sooner. I gathered basic supplies and rushed over. None of my brothers are known for their hospitality, but Isaac and Joaquin happen to be the two worst." She raised her brows at her brother, who now had his head down. "Imagine my surprise when I find one of them here."

Joaquin grunted. Lali couldn't tell if it was in agreement or protest.

Lali's gaze darted between the siblings. Abigail was giving Joaquin the strangest looks. The younger woman shook her head and turned back to Lali with a smile. "I'm so sorry about last night. Isaac didn't inform anyone you were coming. I see you have breakfast." She cut another loaded glance at her brother. "I brought milk, cinnamon rolls and fruit. You can save them for later."

The mountain man grumbled something, and everyone turned to him. He glowered in his sister's direction then sighed. "I should go."

"No," Lali said without thought. "Um, you haven't finished your breakfast." Oscar had stopped eating.

"Yes. All of you should sit back down and keep eating. Sorry I interrupted. I figured with you driving so late you would want to sleep in late."

"We were up when Joaquin arrived with food and offered to cook." From the corner of her eye, her son sunk lower, almost below the counter. Joaquin quietly slid around the island and was signing to Oscar. From her seat, she couldn't make out what he was saying.

"I was telling Oscar—" his voice was low and soothing "—that you're Leo's mom. Oscar likes dinosaurs too. He likes round food and stars. He does not like his food touching, people he doesn't know or loud noises."

Abigail paused while unloading the basket and understanding widened her eyes. "Oh. I'm sorry." She had taken the same low, even tone as

Joaquin. "Y'all don't even know me and I come charging into your space, stomping and yelling."

"We'll survive," she reassured Abigail. "It takes a bit for Oscar to become comfortable in a new place. Joaquin and Luna have been extraordinary with their help."

"Really?" For a second his sister stared at Joaquin as if she didn't know him, then shook her head and went back to her pleasant expression. "My son, Leo, lives on the ranch too. He's about your age. Look at those perfectly round eggs. Your mother is very talented."

"Joaquin made them." Oscar didn't look up, but he spoke clearly.

Abigail made a face. "No. You're making that up."

Oscar blinked and scowled. "I don't lie."

Her hand went to her chest and she opened her mouth to say something, but Joaquin put his hand out to stop her.

He leaned in low to whisper to her son but was loud enough that they could hear. "The thing is, you're the first guest I've ever cooked for, so she's surprised. That's all. She wasn't accusing you of lying."

"We showed up on his doorstep lost," Lali said. "He took care of everything. I can't express how much we appreciate what he's done for us." Now she was repeating herself. Why was she making this so awkward?

"That is one thing I know to be true. He is very good at fixing problems. I'm glad he was there." Abigail cut her brother a side-eye, then turned to Lali. "Here's my number. If you need anything, please don't hesitate to call. We're so excited you accepted Isaac's invitation to survey our cave."

"So, you're pro cave?" Lali couldn't help being pulled into the younger woman's warmth. "Joaquin made it clear most of the family doesn't want the cave explored."

"Joaquin! You have no social skills." She rolled her eyes. "I'm so sorry for my brothers, again. Isaac has led the charge to make sure we do this right. A few of us were so excited that we wanted to jump in and open it to the public. Some—" she cut a glance to her brother, who glowered back at her "—like my grandfather and older brothers would just as soon cover it up and pretend we never found it."

"It's going to bring—" Joaquin stopped talking when he noticed Oscar staring at him. He sighed. "Lali asked if she could see the cave later today. I thought you or Em could watch Oscar."

"Perfect. Leo would love to meet you." Abigail folded the bag she had just emptied and turned to Lali. "Isaac said you wouldn't be able to come out until the new year. What brought you here earlier than you planned?"

"She didn't marry Matias yesterday," Oscar

announced, then put the last bit of toast in his mouth.

A heavy silence filled the air. Heat burned up Lali's neck. "It sounds worse than it is."

Abigail had her hand on her chest. "You had a wedding yesterday?"

"Yes." She glanced at Joaquin. So he hadn't shared her humiliation of showing up on his front porch in a wedding dress. "Joaquin didn't bat an eye at a strange woman showing up in full white bridal regalia. It was a cliché runaway-bride moment."

"You called it off at the last moment? Wow. That had to be hard and brave."

No point in lying to these nice people. "No. I was far from brave. He called it off and I ran without talking to anyone. I promise it was a good thing. I have a little whiplash, but my heart wasn't in it."

That didn't show her in a good light, did it? "It was more of a professional agreement and my parents wanted it to happen." She sealed her lips. The more she talked the worse it sounded.

Abigail nodded. "I get putting yourself in a corner and not knowing how to get out. That happened with my first marriage. But my family was a safe place to land when everything finally fell apart." She rested a comforting hand on Lali's arm. "I hope we can be that for you. I'm here whenever you need to talk."

Joaquin was back to glaring at his sister. "Maybe drop the subject? She probably doesn't want to talk about it to complete strangers."

"Of course. Sorry."

Wanting to reassure her, Lali waved off the concern. "We're good. I really would love to get to work and take my mind off the whole mess." She glanced at Joaquin. "You and Isaac made the right call by not telling anyone outside the family about the cave. All sorts of people will do anything to explore an uncharted cave. Many don't have good intentions. There's no telling what kind of damage they would cause and they could erase millions of years of history."

Her heart beat faster just thinking of the possibilities. "We need to be careful to not destroy what took countless lifetimes to develop and form. There is also so much we can learn and apply to today's problems. Discoveries can change our understanding of Earth and human history, but it has to be done by professionals. We lost two inexperienced farmers in Peru once during a vertical climb. But don't worry. I have all my certifications including wild cave diving. And I'm very selective about my team." Knowing Joaquin's opinion about bringing in a team, she focused on Abigail. "Do you know if you—" She bit her lips to stop talking. Once she got started, she was as bad as Oscar. "Sorry. I get excited about caves."

"I said no teams."

Abigail ignored him. "Don't be. I see why Isaac insisted it had to be you."

"I'm probably the only environmental engineer with specialties in ancient history and cave exploration he knows who also happens to have become available."

"It's a God thing, then. I'm glad you're here." Abigail leaned across the counter and gave her hand a gentle squeeze. "Come over in a couple of hours. See if Oscar is comfortable with us, and Mr. Grumps can take you to the cave. We eat together every Sunday morning and go to church. It's an open invitation, but don't feel you have to come."

"Thank you." She had no clue how to politely decline.

"It would be a good opportunity to meet everyone," Abigail went on.

Then Abigail gasped and reached for Lali's arm. "My fiancé, Kingston Zayas, has the ranch next door. You need to meet his family too. Our ranch has the opening and the first major chamber, but his family's ranch has the majority of the cave under their land." She jumped and clapped. "I know! Tomorrow after church I'm meeting with Letti and Naomi for the Soup in a Jar event. You can come to the Tres Amigos Ranch with me and meet everyone involved."

Oscar slid under the counter again. Abigail covered her mouth. "Sorry. I got excited. I'm getting on to my son all the time about running around like a tornado. He comes by it more honestly than I'd like to admit."

Luna sat up and put her paws on the counter. The mountain man got a rag from the sink. He cleaned the dog's paws and then the counter. He signed for Oscar to sit up and finish his breakfast. After petting the dog, her son signed back that he needed to finish his too. The two went back to eating and ignoring the women as they happily signed back and forth.

What was happening? Her son never communicated with anyone on this level but her.

Abigail leaned forward on her elbows. "They seem to be getting along well. Joaquin has a good heart. He is the grumpiest of the DeLeons and the most antisocial."

Lali raised her brow. "More so than Isaac?"

"In a different way, but yes. He wasn't always the hermit on the hillside. Family folklore says as a child and teen he was the most outgoing and sociable of the litter. Now he's the man on the dark side of the moon."

"I find that hard to believe. He has gone above

and beyond to make us feel welcome. Well, from the minute he found out Isaac had invited us. The first few minutes were touch and go. Then there's the cave thing. He doesn't seem happy about us being here for the cave."

"Maybe there's a body snatcher? The anti-cave thing is on brand, but venturing out of his lair to engage with other humans and making breakfast? I wouldn't have believed it if I hadn't seen it." The pretty woman grinned.

"You know I can hear you," Joaquin rumbled from across the island.

His sister winked at her. "I'm grateful he was there for you last night and this morning. Now about the soup jar party. Will you come?"

Because her parents went where the grants were, Lali had grown up traveling to small, out-of-the-way villages and large urban areas. She had experienced many unfamiliar celebrations from different cultures, but this was new. "What's a soup jar party?"

"We assemble layers of dry ingredients in large mason jars along with handmade Christmas cards."

"For gifts?"

"Kind of. In two weeks, we'll gather at the church with other members and divide into groups. Each gets a list of homes to visit of those who need some extra TLC and holiday cheer.

We'll sing a couple of Christmas songs and pass out the jars." She glanced at Oscar. "But you don't have to join us for that unless you want to. Isaac helps with the jars, but he doesn't do caroling."

"Thank you for the invitation. I'll think about it."

Abigail's face lit up. "In three weeks, Kingston and I will be getting married on the property line between the two ranches. You'll still be here, right?" She moved to her brother and wrapped her arms around his. "The two families will be one big happy family then."

Joaquin opened his mouth, and the friendly Abigail glared daggers at him. "Don't you dare say anything."

"What? I'm happy for you and Kingston, but your happy ending doesn't erase generations of family distrust."

Had she put herself and her son into the midst of a land dispute? She'd seen those turn the best ideas sideways. She wasn't sure she had the energy to deal with that kind of family drama.

Maybe she should just go back and work things out with her parents.

But her priority right now was finding a safe, calm place to land where she could support her son and figure out what came next. The mountain cowboy was way too distracting for them both and in no way was he safe. She was tired of walking on a tightrope.

* * *

Joaquin didn't like the idea of Lali spending too much time alone with the Zayases. There was a tentative treaty between the families due to their son loving his sister so much. Whenever they were together it was easy to see how Kingston adored and respected her. He had left his business and home in Dallas to make one here with her.

But it didn't erase the painful past. It had nothing to do with Kingston, but grudges and memories ran as deep as their family roots.

"No harm in getting to know the other half of the cave owners. Please say yes," Abigail practically begged.

"Abigail, back off." He hadn't meant to snap at her. Taking a deep breath, he tried again. "They had a rough night, and running out to meet strangers is stressful for most people who aren't extroverts on steroids."

His baby sister's face fell. "Oh. He's right. I'm sorry."

"The idea's a good one. I'll think about it," Lali offered.

Oscar leaned a little into him as he took the last bite of his still-round egg. Why did this boy trust him? There was nothing trustworthy about him.

The old yearning for having kids made an unwelcome wave for attention. It was safer to focus on his nephew and niece.

The kid probably associated him with Luna. That's all this bond was. Kids liked dogs.

"What do you think, Joaquin?" His sister and Abigail were waiting for an answer to a question he hadn't heard. He turned away from them to put his plate in the sink. Being silent and surly had its benefits.

Abigail smiled. "You were saying last weekend that Luna needed more field testing. She seems really connected to Oscar. If you brought her to the soup jar party, it would help you both."

He closed his eyes. She had been trying to get him to engage with community events. Now she had a new angle. She saw a weakness and was going straight for it.

He sighed. "No. If I can't make progress with her training she'll go to go back to Valerie the first of January."

"She's not yours?" Oscar asked. He slid to the ground and hugged her.

"No. I work with an organization in San Antonio that rescues retired or dismissed military dogs. I take the dogs to train for six months to a year, then recommend the best situation to place the dog. I specialize in dogs that help veterans with PTSD. Luna hasn't shown promise." He stared at the dog and then made eye contact with Lali. "Until last night. She wasn't responding the way I needed her to. But she's a different dog around him. She clearly prefers kids to adults." Maybe he could use this connection to help them both.

Oscar slapped the counter. "I want to help. So, she was fired by the army? Was Shadow fired too?"

"He was officially retired due to an injury. Shadow's mine. We were paired together. That's how I found out about the program. They rescue military dogs and pair them with veterans that need support, some physical and others mental."

"What happens if they fire her again?" Oscar sounded very concerned.

"I'm not sure. All of the dogs I've trained have gone on to be successfully paired with someone." Luna was such a smart dog. Admitting defeat did not sit well with him. Maybe there was another way to find success with her. "I do have an idea though. Since you know sign language you could help me test her. We can see if she is different with kids." His gaze switched to Oscar's mom. "Can he do that?"

Joaquin stayed still as Lali studied him. He could see her question about why he needed Shadow, but she was too polite to ask. Not all wounds had visible scars.

He also buried the urge to ask her about her scars. Asking her would permit her to ask him. It also would mean he cared. Caring for people who waltzed in and out of his life wasn't worth the risk.

Abigail came to his side. "He does amazing work helping dogs and soldiers find their perfect partners." She gave him a side hug. "Does this mean I can count on all of you to be at our soup jar party?"

"I didn't say that. I was thinking here or at the house. I'm coming for breakfast in the morning then church. It's a normal routine for Luna so it would be interesting to see if she reacts differently with him." He looked to Lali for her response.

"I'm all for it if Oscar agrees."

"I agree!"

Joaquin gave a curt nod. "I need to cover basic signs with you and Luna. Can we do it now?"

Oscar stood and smiled.

Joaquin went to the door. "Let me get her vest. When the vest is on she knows it's time to work."

By the time he came back Oscar was sitting by the fireplace. He held out the vest and walked Oscar through the steps of putting it on and what it meant when she was wearing it.

The women had stayed in the kitchen, cleaning up the breakfast dishes. As he went through basic commands and ensured Luna followed Oscar, his sister and Lali chatted as they worked.

He heard his name a couple of times, but he

couldn't split his attention, so he tried to block them out.

Then Lali laughed and all his blockades crumbled. His attention was drawn to the kitchen area.

Big mistake. After studying Lali, he accidentally made eye contact with his sister. She raised her brow, and he turned his gaze back to Oscar and Luna.

Luna was bonding faster with the boy than he had ever known a dog to bond. She acted as if they had always been a team, and Oscar communicated confidently.

He would have to call Valerie and ask her about the best course of action. His job was to evaluate and train the dogs she sent him. Then, with his recommendation, she paired the dogs with a veteran. The dog always finished their training with that person.

It wasn't the usual way of doing things, but they had an unblemished success rate.

Would Lali want a service dog for Oscar, and could she afford Luna? The dogs he worked with went to veterans and Valerie had connections to grants for them to help with the cost.

If Lali agreed to take the dog maybe he could waive his trainer fee. Some things happened at the right time and place for a reason. Maybe God had brought Lali and Oscar to his door for them to meet Luna. That made sense. It had nothing to do with him.

In the best-case scenario, he could hand over a successful Luna when Lali and Oscar left, and then he would head to Mexico.

Oscar walked across the room with Luna at his heel. He stopped and told her to lie down. She kept her gaze glued to the boy, and after a few tries, she did everything he asked of her. Oscar had the biggest smile on his face when he looked at Joaquin for approval.

Joaquin brought his flat hand to his chin, lowered it into his other hand and tapped his fist. He mouthed, "Good job."

The new team crossed the room to him, and he rubbed Luna behind her ear. She enjoyed that more than treats. Looking up, he found the women watching him and his skin grew too tight for his body.

Abigail turned to him. "After church you're coming to the Tres Amigos?"

He shook his head. "Nope. I'll meet y'all at the main house in the morning and go to church, but that's it." He didn't think he could handle any more contact. He had Oscar help him remove Luna's vest. He signed a goodbye and left with the dogs.

Fresh air and a good run were in his immediate future. Yes. He'd spend the rest of the day outside with the horses. The yearlings needed his attention.

"Joaquin?" His sister's voice stopped his escape as he reached his truck door.

He didn't turn around or say a word, just waited.

"What are you doing?" Her tone was unusually sharp.

"Going to the horse barn and pasture. The yearlings need time in the round pen lunging with blankets." He pressed his lips together to stop babbling. He knew that wasn't what she was asking about. "I need to get all of that done if I am escorting Dr. Kan to the cave later today."

"Wow. That was more explanation than I've ever gotten from you." She leaned on the hood of his truck to put herself in his line of vision. "But I didn't need to know your schedule. Why did you bring them food and cook breakfast so early this morning and then—" she was being overly dramatic with the last word "—you offer to help take her to the cave. You." She pointed at him. "Mr. I-Don't-Like-People-Not-Related-to-Me. What's going on in your lone-wolf brain?"

"They showed up on my doorstep. What was I supposed to do? Ignore them?"

"No. But you've gone way beyond your comfort zone for two strangers. And I saw the way you interacted with them. You smiled. A real smile I've only seen around your niece and nephew."

She made it sound like an accusation. "I don't know what you're talking about."

"You know she's only here for a month or so, right? Isaac told me she's teaching at the University in Mexico City for the spring semester. She'll be leaving mid-January at the latest."

"Good. I don't want her or anyone else on the ranch." He blew out a puff of air. "I have things to do." He stepped up into his truck.

She came around. "I know about Celeste and her son, Ethan. You keep pulling back further and further away from us. I don't want to see you hurt more than you already are."

He frowned. "How do you know about them?" He'd only told one person. He couldn't believe Cyrus had betrayed him.

"Cyrus was worried about you. He talked to me. I don't think anyone else knows, but there has been a huge shift in how you interact with people. Cyrus has seen it the most. I don't think it's in your core nature to be a recluse. I've been praying—"

He snorted. "Give your prayers to someone who needs them."

"We all need prayers. Joaquin—"

He cut her off. "People change. I'm not the same kid I was. Too much…" He stopped mid-sentence and looked at his baby sister.

She was the best of them, a true survivor who still had her heart intact. "Thank you for being worried about me, but I'm fine. I'm good with my life just the way it is. I'm not looking for any sort of relationship with Dr. Kan or her son. What you see is the unexpected connection between her son and Luna. I'm feeling that out. It could be what the boy and dog need. I'm not going to ignore it because I don't want to be around strangers. God put her on my doorstep for a reason and I want to do what's best for Luna. It might be Oscar." He adjusted his hat. "No need to be all dramatic."

"You need to stop running."

"I'm not." He sighed. "I have things to do."

She nodded and stepped back. "I'll see you tomorrow morning."

He closed the door and started the engine. There was no need to make tomorrow's interactions longer by going to that jar party. He would never admit it to his little sister, but she was right. Dr Xitlali Kan and her son were dangerous to his well-balanced life.

Taking her to the cave later today would get her closer to leaving. The ranch was a sanctuary for his family. He knew how to play nice when their peace was at risk.

Chapter Five

Lali parked her car at the end of the dirt road. "Where to now?" The rocky hillside was covered in a diverse species of trees and shrubs. Scanning the area for any signs of a path was the easiest way to avoid Joaquin.

The friendly guy from this morning was gone. He had expected to drive his truck and wasn't thrilled about riding in her car, but even he acknowledged it was ridiculous to repack all her equipment and climbing gear. The trip along the barely-there road to the opposite side of the ranch was done in heavy silence.

He pointed to the left and grunted. It might have been a word, but she didn't recognize it. Opening her door, she went to the back of her Range Rover.

Both dogs joined them. Luna still looked as if she was put out that Oscar wasn't with her. It had been strange leaving Oscar with a woman she'd only met this morning, but it was great sense of relief when he'd established a quick connection with Leo. It probably helped that Leo had an uncle on the spectrum.

Maybe God had brought them to the right place. She glanced at Joaquin.

Nothing could be perfect.

She had made sure to do her daily devotion after the DeLeons had left the house, a practice she had allowed to slip lately. Monthly devotion would be more accurate if she was generous. How could she know what God wanted from her if she wasn't taking the time to listen?

Joaquin was leaning on Shadow.

"Is something wrong?" she asked.

His fingers curled into the big black dog's thick coat. "No." He adjusted his hat. "Oscar was okay with Abigail and Leo?"

Okay, her son was a subject on which they could stand on common ground. "Yes. It was great seeing him interact with other kids. Emma was there too. Oscar hasn't had many friends his age so the idea that he could have one is encouraging."

Opening the split tailgate, she pulled her large backpack and bags closer. Not knowing the cave, she wasn't sure what gear would be needed today. "Would you mind carrying a backpack? After today I'll have a better idea of what I need so I won't have to take it all."

"No problem."

"Oscar asked about Luna. I told him he'd see her tomorrow." She smiled at the dog. "She looked very disappointed when I came out of the house without him."

Joaquin frowned at the Akita, who was lying down with her muzzle resting between her front paws. "Stop pouting. You just met him yesterday."

Lali laughed and pulled out a helmet for him. "Poor girl. Maybe she has abandonment issues?"

"Could be. She was a rescue with high potential. She's trained to find explosives and weapons. But she was fired on her first day when she was distracted by a couple of kids. She's smart and Valerie was hoping she would make a good service dog. But she might be my first failure."

"She's amazing with Oscar. He's never handled new locations and people this well. I think it has to do with her." Lali handed him the helmet.

He raised an eyebrow and tipped his black cowboy hat to her. "I'm good."

The hat looked good on him, but she would never ever admit that out loud. "This is about safety and practicality. Caves are very dark and you also need your hands so..." She tapped the light on the helmet. "Illumination that you don't have to hold."

"I've got a flashlight that works just fine."

She shook her head. "Multiple sources of light

are preferred. But no one goes into my site without a helmet. The only predictability about cave exploring is it's unpredictable."

"It's my ranch. And I thrive on the unpredictable."

He gave her a smile that made her heart beat faster. What was she, a hormonal teenager? "In a cave it can lead to death. I don't like that kind of paperwork." She looked him up and down. "Plus, there is no way I could drag you out of that cave if you were unconscious."

His smile just became more ridiculous. "I don't know. You seem pretty resourceful."

With a sigh she let him change the subject, for now. She went through the packs and explained the purpose of each item then finished with the helmet. And told him a few stories of climbs that went wrong because of pride and stubbornness.

Holding out the helmet to him again, she waited for him to take it. "Since it's just you and me you're putting us both in danger."

He narrowed his eyes for a heartbeat, then took off his hat and ran his fingers through his hair.

When the helmet was in place, she pressed her lips together to keep the smile from going too big. He probably wouldn't appreciate it. Inside she did a little I-won dance.

Keeping her face neutral, she turned to the tree line. "So, where to now?"

"It's a good long hike this way. Hope you're up for it." His large frame went right past her and into the trees. The dogs stayed close. Luna turned and looked at her as if questioning her commitment.

As he zigzagged through the trees and over large rocks pushing up through the ground, she followed close behind. "Most caves worth documenting are hard to get to. I've been in Austria, Mexico and Croatia to name a few. A couple of them were overnight hikes."

He just kept climbing, acting as if she hadn't said a word. Then he stopped. Standing on the edge of a huge rock, he turned. Pulling herself up, she moved next to him.

From here, they could see over the trees. The valley and hills spread across the wide horizon were breathtaking. To think his family had lived here for so many generations boggled the mind. Her father talked about his Indigenous roots and the history of ancient people, but there really wasn't anything tangible in her family. Not like this ranch and the DeLeons' personal history.

"It's amazing thinking about the untouched history right under our feet." The baritone of his voice pulled her out of the past. "Another reason," he continued, "I have my doubts about doing this."

"But it's that untouched history that can help solve problems we face today."

"Problems we created." He was quick to respond.

"Maybe. But think about the things we've learned over the years, and the changes already being made. It's a rare opportunity to listen and learn. Hopefully to discover and grow." A gust of cold wind swirled around them. Pulling her coat tighter around her, she studied the vast landscape. That wisdom was needed in her personal life as well.

He sighed and jumped off the rock. "It's over here."

Behind them to the left were two twisted giant live oak trees about ten feet apart. The roots of the largest pushed between slabs of limestone, slowly shoving the rock out of the way for probably a hundred years. That was the kind of persistence she needed with her parents.

Joaquin knelt and lifted a screen of grass and leaves off a trapdoor anchored with a concrete frame. "The original cave where Leo fell in is about forty yards that way." He pointed behind her. "It has a ledge then drops about fifty feet. We were able to rappel down, but the situation proved too dangerous for repeated access. We found these stair-like rocks in the next chamber over. To make exploring easier, Lucas, Isaac and Kingston installed some lighting, though sparingly. It's powered by the solar panel in the top of the trees. Issac was adamant about preserving the natural environment and preventing any significant changes."

"That's smart." A heavy black cord ran down the tree trunk into the hole. She stepped closer, gazing into the opening. After the first several feet it was too dark to make out any details. "Cave environments are very stable. Any shift in humidity or temps can change the conditions."

He grunted. "Which is another argument for sealing it up to let it do what it's doing. As soon as we stepped inside, we interfered."

"Interruptions can be minimized. Areas that are fragile can be identified and restricted, but much of the cave will consist of dirt, rock and water. The potential of what we can learn is—" She cut herself off. "Sorry, I'm just super excited. I understand you're not fully behind me being here, but I appreciate the chance."

He stepped over the manmade curb and descended downward. At first there were a few rocks, then a short slope. Next was a rock ledge that went down into another ledge like huge steps that had been made for giants.

They turned on their lights. "I'm sure you know this, but I've had team members forget that wild creatures claim this space as their home. Rattlesnakes love rocky caves, so watch where you put your hands and feet."

A grunt was the only response she received. She bent her knees and carefully angled her feet to control and maintain her balance as the angle of the incline became steeper.

"There's a rope here," he offered.

Finding it, she stayed very focused to make sure she put her feet and hands in a safe place. Snakes were just one of the many animals that would seek shelter here.

When the ground leveled out, Joaquin went to the cave wall and connected two cords. Instantly the area was illuminated past their headlamps. She stopped breathing.

This put all the show caves in Texas to shame. The height of the ceiling had to be sixty feet in some spots. The chamber was enormous. In the center was a column so wide she and Joaquin would not be able to join hands around it. Clusters of smaller ones surrounded it.

And the ceiling. A curved path of stalactite hung like fragile icicles huddled along the side of the cave, and a long line trailed across the center. Along the floor large groupings of stalagmites reached up toward them, as if God had built His own cathedral.

At the back of the cave her gaze stopped. "That's the most impressive example of flowstone I've ever encountered." It was the highest point of the ceiling and huge sheets of calcium carbonate draped over ledges and cascaded into beautiful rows. A shallow pool of water was on the ground. She carefully made her way to it. Joaquin gave the dogs an order to stay, then followed her.

"It's like a fossilized waterfall."

"Em calls it the Frozen Frio Falls. It's a little over eighty feet tall."

They stood next to each other in silence. Slow drips of water filled the space.

"Is this the largest chamber?"

"Nope." He hunched and balanced on his heels to study the clear water. "The next chamber is twice as big but not as many formations. Connected to that one is a smaller one. There are more openings and crevices that might lead to other open spaces, but we haven't had the time or equipment to enter safely. There are small streams that run through the other chambers. We think the river is below the third chamber."

"Two more and one is bigger than this?" There was no way she could do a complete survey by herself but now was not the time to point that out. She wanted his support.

This morning Joaquin had been so great, she'd thought she had a friend. Now he was cold and distant.

Maybe Isaac could help. He seemed to have an influence on her mountain man.

Nope. No. Not her mountain man. Just a rancher that owned a cave.

This was not personal. It couldn't be. He stood and stretched his shoulders. She had never been around a man that had such a strong physical presence.

It was a primitive part of her brain that was reacting to him. She was smarter than her base biological instincts. She had to be.

Joaquin closed his eyes to the sight of Dr. Kan standing in awe in front of the flowstone. She was studying the mammoth formation the way other women might be mesmerized by royal crowns. It was more than the glint in her eyes. She used her whole body as she took in each detail of the cave.

It was her job; she wasn't anything special. She glanced at him with a questioning expression. He must be mumbling to himself again. He forced a smile.

He had a job too: to be a good steward of the land his family has vowed to protect for generations.

"This is just a quick look. We need to move on. It's a tight fit to the larger chamber." He moved to the crevices where two giant boulders pushed against each other.

Joining him, she put a hand reverently on one of the rocks that towered over her, as if to comfort it or encourage the thing to tell her its story. "At some point in the cave's history there was a collapse." Her voice was soft and soothing.

"Yeah. They aren't moving. We'll have to squeeze through." He ducked his head to investigate the small dark path. "You don't have a problem with tight damp places, do you?"

She raised a brow. "Do I need to show you my résumé?"

"Right." He had to chuckle. Most people avoided challenging him. He liked that she called him out. "It's part of what you love about cave exploring."

"If you were able to get through, I don't foresee me having any problems." Her gaze darted across the width of his shoulders.

"Yeah. Being the biggest of the litter, I was the last to go. There's one spot we have to get down into an army crawl. But I must admit, when we clear the opening it's pretty magical."

"Do you need Shadow?"

"No. They'll wait for us."

"Then let's go." With a wide smile and a spark in her eyes she nodded. He turned to move forward. He had to agree that having both hands free from holding a flashlight was so much better, but he wasn't ready to admit that to her.

Once he cleared the passage he stood and flipped the lights on. Behind him a feminine gasp told him she was out also. An unwarranted pride filled his chest. Dr. Kan had seen the world's most amazing caves and theirs had her gasping.

"Nice, right?" he asked.

"It's like stepping onto another planet."

Tiny crystals shimmered in the light. Intricate formations crawled up the wall and across the ceiling. The ground gently sloped downward, about the length of a football field. "It's taken a million years for calcium to shape curtains this large. And the straws. That's the largest cluster I've even seen and it's unbroken."

With her phone out she walked along the wall taking pictures. A shallow stream ran along the wall beside her. "I can only imagine what kind of animals live in this ecosystem. Joaquin, this is stunning. How far does this one go? Is that another opening at the far end?"

"Yes. It's a very small pocket. It leads to a river below. We haven't gone the whole way. Without the right equipment or experience we felt it was too dangerous." He pointed to an opening above them. "That's the original shaft Leo fell into. Thankfully there's a ledge. It's not a safe way to get in and out. We rappelled down to here then found it went up to a better entry point. Right above us is the property line between the two ranches."

"The other ranch is the one that wants to open it to the public?"

"They want to go deeper and see if there are other viable chambers to turn into a tourist destination. They're even talking about a gift shop and events. I don't think it's worth the risk."

"Finding a large, easily navigable cave like this is rare. I agree it must be protected. But you might have only touched a small piece of it. With the right equipment and team we could get—"

"No teams," he cut her off.

"Joaquin, I understand you don't want people to tread all over the ranch. The team would be small, and handpicked. They'll sign anything you want them to sign. The people I choose to work with get the importance of protecting this space. I wouldn't bring anyone in that would—"

"No." He said it as firmly as he could without yelling. "Isaac said we could trust you and we agreed to trust him on this. It's only you or nothing."

"There's no way one person can do this."

He shrugged. "Then it's not going to be surveyed. We'll seal the hole. I'm already afraid people are going to start nosing around. Leo loves telling his story of falling into a cave. Some have already asked. We've been saying it was just a small cave on the side of a rocky ledge. If more people start coming in, people will notice. It's a small town."

"You have something unique here and whatever you decide to do with it is your right, but it should be studied. It holds answers to questions we didn't even know to ask."

He crossed his arms. "Do you want to spend your time arguing with me or do you want to see the rest of the cave?"

She pulled the corner of her bottom lip between her teeth. The desire to argue with him burned in her eyes, but after a moment she shook her head. "I'll do the best I can without a team for now."

Camera in hand, she turned away from him and took more pictures.

At times she would stop to write and make sketches in a notebook. She had a handheld device that took readings of the air.

It was probably unfair to expect her to survey it alone, but more people on the ranch was the last thing he wanted. Without any natural light it was easy to lose track of time. He looked at his watch. "How long do you want to be in here?"

She didn't acknowledge him but lay flat on the ground to inspect the underside of an overhang. He no longer existed in her world. He went to her side and balanced himself on his heels. "How much longer, doc? I'll set the alarm on my watch."

"Oh no." She looked at her phone. "I told Oscar that I'd be back in two hours. I only have about thirty more minutes."

"Do you want to see the smaller cave before we leave?"

Reluctantly she shook her head. "I want to go back to the first chamber. I'll explore the other areas when I have more time."

The climb up to the first chamber was steady. Once there he sat with the dogs. It was fascinating to watch her study the cave, but being fascinated by Dr. Kan was not a good thing.

He pulled his pocket notebook out and focused on the plan he and the ranchers in Mexico had been working on. The original longhorns were something else on his list that needed to be protected.

His alarm went off. "Time's up." He stood.

She sighed. "There's so much to—"

"No. Team." Each word was clear. "We aren't budging on that."

"We? Who is that group made up of? Isn't there another party that might agree with me? Some people I'll meet with tomorrow?"

He narrowed his eyes. Was she threatening him? "There is, but they don't have access to the cave. My grandfather will never allow a team on his property." He extended his arm to the path going up to ground level.

With a quick turn she put her back to him, took the rope in hand and started the final climb up.

He signaled the dogs to go up and then followed. When he pulled himself over the last rock the cool November air filled his lungs. She was putting her gear in her backpack. He closed and locked the trapdoor.

There, he had done his job. She had seen the cave and was safely back on ground level. "I'm going to check on the pastures. I'll get my truck later."

"I can drive you." She looked a little confused by his decision to walk. Good, because she had him a lot confused.

"No." He pulled his notebook out. "I have a few projects to check on."

"What—" Her phone rang. She glanced at it. "It's my parents. I haven't talked to them since..." She waved her hand around as if that explained her missing words. The phone went silent. After a pause it started again. "I can't avoid them forever." The ringing stopped again, only to resume less than a minute later.

With a sigh she accepted the call, hit the speaker icon and stared at the sky. "Hola."

"Hola? Hola! That's all you have to say?" A women's shrill voice screamed across the air.

He stepped away to give her privacy, but she looked at him in a panic. She wanted him to stay?

Needing something to do, he crouched over the equipment and studied it, or tried to.

The mother was yelling in Spanish. He really tried not to listen, but he caught the words *impulsive*, *reckless* and *irresponsible*. Lali argued it was the right thing to do. She told her mom she had to find her own path. But her mother wasn't listening and cut her off.

Oscar's name was said several times. Lali moved to an outcropping of gray rocks and sat on the tallest one. Her mother went on to accuse Lali of being a selfish daughter and mother.

Luna left his side and went to Lali. The dog rested her chin on the dust-covered cargo pants.

The doctor went quiet as her mother barged on with her commentary. He turned his full gaze to her. She had her forehead resting on her free hand, the turquoise climbing glove still on.

She lifted her face to the sky, but her eyes were tightly closed. Her throat moved as she struggled to swallow. Pressing her lips tightly together, she twisted them back and forth. She was fighting not to cry.

"Mija, you need to grow up and come back to fix what you have broken. This will bring down your career. We've worked too hard for you to rip everything apart on a self-centered whim."

A tear slipped past her lashes, and she dropped her head to utter defeat. "Matias doesn't want to be Oscar's father, and I don't want to be Matias's wife."

"Mija, it's Popi." Her father joined the conversation. "Come home so we can minimize the damage."

She curled into herself.

Should he do something? What? He didn't deal with his own trauma well. He had no clue how to help her.

He'd known her for less than twenty-four hours but this morning in the kitchen she'd seemed very straightforward and devoted to her son, not impulsive or irresponsible. Then again, she'd shown up at midnight in a wedding dress on his front doorstep.

This was way too complicated for him. He turned away from her and ran his fingers through Shadow's coat. Luna was still with her, offering more comfort than he could.

He should make a call to Javier. The older man had taken the lead for the ranchers in Mexico. They were having problems with the grazing lands. That was something he could help with.

"Come home, now," her mother yelled.

Joaquin's stomach churned. He hated this kind of drama and didn't want it in his life. He should walk away but it would be rude to just leave her. Then again, he couldn't imagine she wanted him to witness her distress. Leaving someone in pain went against everything in him.

"No. I can't. I'm staying here. Don't call again if you're just going to bring the same arguments. I'll be back in Mexico City in time for the new term. I just— Momi? Popi?" She stared down at her phone.

Her gaze met Joaquin's and he found sheer devastation. Luna placed her paws on Lali's thigh then looked at Joaquin as if he should do something. Lali stood. "They hung up on me."

He joined her by the rocks. "It's going to be okay." He had no clue if that was right, but he didn't know what else to say.

She leaned forward and pressed her forehead to his shoulder. One arm went around her and she sobbed into his jacket.

Looking over the pastures below, he prayed for the right thing to say or do. He tightened his hold a little and remained silent.

After a bit she stepped back. Shadow was sitting next to him and Luna had lain down between them. The golden Akita now looked up at Lali, who crouched down and met her at eye level. A little time passed as she loved on Luna. Then she stood.

"That was embarrassing. And the reason I was avoiding them. I don't know what I'm going to do."

"Right now, you have a place to stay and a job

to do. I have enough experience to know you're a good mom. Doing it on your own is tough, but it's better than compromising your well-being or your son's."

The urge to hold her was powerful. It felt too natural and... He should put as much distance between them as possible, but he couldn't just abandon her. "Do you mind driving me to the main house? I need to talk to my grandfather, and you can get Oscar."

He had a feeling she needed her son right now, and he needed to keep his arms next to his sides.

"Yes, of course. Thank you."

It was time for visit the ranches in Mexico. That was a safe place to go.

Chapter Six

Joaquin stood at the back entrance of his family's home, his hand on the screen door, but he wasn't ready to open it. The house had been built in 1894, and in its day was a true showstopper. His grandparents had modernized it in the mid-sixties.

Nothing had changed much since then, and his grandmother's and mother's choices remained in the home. It was an eclectic mix of the generations that had called it home.

His grandfather had raised them here and now his oldest brother and little sister were raising the next generation within these walls.

The original large blocks of limestone held all the love and grief collected over the years. For a moment he heard his mother's laughter as the screen door banged shut. They were running to the pasture with their flashlights and jars.

She had told them that fireflies used their light to talk to each other. He and his siblings would flash their lights on and off as one, and the fireflies had repeated their pattern.

He smiled. Their mother had convinced them they could communicate with fireflies. Did Abigail remember that? She had been so little. He'd make sure to share the experience with Leo.

Oscar would love it too. Joaquin jerked his hand away from the memory-worn handle and stepped away from the door. Those bittersweet memories always jolted him with pain, a pain he'd worked to evade. He needed to keep distance from Oscar. He didn't want to get hurt or have the boy feel rejected when they left.

"Luna. Shadow." Isaac was walking toward the house, too, and greeted the dogs first. He bent down and ran his hands over them, checking their eyes. Joaquin would have been offended if he didn't know this was how his baby brother interacted with all domestic animals.

Isaac stood but his gaze stayed on the dogs. "They look healthy and happy."

"I like to think they are." He grinned at Isaac.

"Just because you think it doesn't make it happen. Pet care is a responsibility that must be taken seriously, and they both have a traumatic past."

"That's true." He sighed with resolve and opened the door for his brother.

"Sorry. You already know that. I don't have to tell you."

"No harm done," he assured his little brother.

They stepped out of the mud room and into the kitchen.

"Tio Isaac. Tio Joaquin! We have company and Oscar says he knows Luna," said Leo as he ran over.

Joaquin took Luna to Oscar. It was like reuniting long-lost siblings. "He does. Luna asked to come see him."

"Tio Joaquin, dogs don't talk." Leo was all smiles, but then he blinked and stared at Luna. "They don't, right?"

"They have a language," Isaac offered. "When you're around them a lot, you can understand what they're saying."

"Really?" Leo faced Oscar. "Does she talk to you?"

Grinning from ear to ear, Oscar nodded.

Joaquin couldn't stop smiling. The boys were so full of joy and excitement. He glanced up and found his usually happy sister frowning at him. When they made eye contact, she raised her brows.

That killed his good mood. So, she had questions. Inquiries he'd rather not explore.

Taking a bowl of cut fruit to the table, Abigail brushed his shoulders. "Change your mind about the soup jar party?"

He didn't have to justify his choices, so he ignored her and sat at the end of the table next to his grandfather. Shadow sat in the corner closest to him and Luna curled up at Oscar's feet.

Oscar was telling Leo how when Luna wore her vest she was working. They couldn't treat her like a pet. "Since she's not wearing the vest, we can play with her."

Isaac gave everyone an info dump on working dogs and how they impacted the development of civilization.

Joaquin kept his gaze away from Lali. He was not going to ask her how she was doing. He was not going to the soup jar party.

His grandfather cleared his throat. "Everyone needs to settle down if we're going to make it to church on time. Let me bless our day as we get started so that we can eat and get going."

In an instant, his family lowered their heads, and their hands reached out so they made a complete circle. Joaquin loved this moment the most. Everyone was connected and safe.

His grandfather's words of blessing and gratitude settled over him as the chaos turned into quiet reflection.

It felt right that Lali and Oscar were here too. He tightened his lids and lowered his head. *God, strengthen my heart and give me peace to accept my life as it is. Why do I always crave more?*

Tito closed his prayer over the family. Ending

his own prayer, Joaquin lifted his head. Amens went around the table and the room was quiet for the next few minutes as they ate.

They finished breakfast and headed to church.

As they filled their family pew, he found comfort in the music that swirled around him. He sat in the pew before Lali and Oscar so he wouldn't be tempted to stare at them. If he could keep them out of his line of vision, maybe he could keep them out of his mind.

Both dogs sat at the end of their pews. Shadow kept nudging his hand. The dog was worried about him. He petted him, reassuring him that he was distracted but okay.

With the vest on, everyone knew it meant the dogs were working and not to be approached or petted. That was one of the nice things about the small, tight-knit community of Rio Bella.

It had been easy to educate people about the service dogs he trained. Of course, the locals also knew all about his history. Lali and Oscar were causing a stir. He could tell people were curious as to who they really were and why Oscar had Luna.

He sighed and glanced at his watch. It was almost time to go home. He had had enough of peopleing today.

After the last hymn he made his way to the door. The temperature had dropped almost twenty degrees while they'd been inside.

"How did it get so cold so fast?" Lali pulled her light sweater closer to her.

Abigail laughed. "Welcome to Texas. A cold front can roll in without much warning, but it leaves just as fast. Usually."

He moved ahead of the women and followed the boys as they ran across the green lawn and jumped over a rock-lined path.

Leo laughed at something and pulled Oscar toward the parking lot. Luna stayed right with them. They were too close to the vehicles that had started moving out. He made his way closer to them.

A gust of wind hit Joaquin in the face and a loud boom went off. The boys were in danger. Without a thought, he covered Leo and Oscar and pressed them to the side of his truck, protecting them with his body.

Lila hadn't prepared herself to see Joaquin again this morning. His presence was all-consuming. He took up too much space without even trying. Maybe it was just his size. She was used to being around men that were closer to her height. The academic world was not known for its warrior-type personalities and builds.

What was she doing? She put her hand to her forehead. Just two days ago, she ran from her wedding. All she needed right now was to clear her head and heart and hit a restart button for her life.

Of course, there had never been anything romantic between her and Mateo. Just a business arrangement between colleagues from the very beginning. Her parents had initiated the union.

Joaquin was a completely different type of man than she was used to. It was curiosity, which was the same thing that had got her into trouble with her first marriage. Of course, Joaquin was nothing like Avery either. Avery had been immature and selfish.

Abigail came up next to her and wrapped an arm around hers. "I'm so glad you were brave enough to join us this morning."

Conversation floated around them as they walked across the trimmed churchyard to the parking lot.

Lali imagined how it felt to come home after being gone for too long, warm and safe. The feeling was unexpected.

Dreams of a large, open, fun family had been hidden deep in her imagination. The guilt of wanting more than the wonderful opportunities her parents had given her made her feel like a bad daughter.

It was just that the academic world was so stuffy and competitive at times. They loved the pressure and thrived on it. Everyone had to prove their intelligence and protect the information they'd gathered for research. It exhausted her.

She felt more at home with this family than she'd ever felt with hers. It made her a very ungrateful daughter.

And what was the deal with being attracted to the silent mountain man when she had just taken off a wedding dress?

She shook her head. There were a few issues she needed to work through.

Abigail bumped her shoulder. "Everything okay? I don't think you heard a word I've said in the last few minutes." Joaquin's sister was younger than her but seemed to have it together.

Abigail smiled at her now, with concern, no judgment. "You seem deep in thought. Lucas will warn you it's a dangerous place to go."

Lali couldn't help but chuckle. "I most definitely need to figure some things out. In the past forty-eight hours my life has turned upside down and I just really appreciate your family welcoming Oscar and me. It's amazing how you've all made us feel like we belong here."

Abigail gave her a side hug. "Believe me, I totally get life throwing you a curveball so fast you don't even have time to duck. I've been there myself, but God has a way of putting us where we need to be if we take the time to pay attention and listen."

There was a loud pop, then the sound of a body crashing into a car. Abigail stiffened and Lali turned to look.

Joaquin's black dog, Shadow, was on his back legs, with his paws pressing Joaquin against the car. His nose was on his face. Joaquin huddled against the truck, the boys under him. Luna wedged herself in between the boys.

Abigail started rushing, then stopped and took a breath. She grabbed Lali's hand and moved to the truck at a slower, calm pace. Lali followed, scanning the area for danger. What had happened to cause Joaquin to cover the boys?

Cyrus and Lucas casually moved in front of their brother, blocking him and the boys from curious eyes. "That car's backfire must have triggered him. It's been a while since it's happened," Abigail said in a low voice for Lali only. She smiled at people as they passed them.

Rigo, their grandfather, had a hand on Joaquin's shoulder. Oscar had his head buried in Luna's fur. Joaquin slowly stood. Blinking, he looked lost.

His gaze shifted to the boys and then he knelt in front of them. He talked to them so quietly she couldn't hear what he said.

Rigo stood back. "Are you okay, mijo?"

The tall mountain man picked up his nephew and held him close. "I'm good. Didn't mean to scare the boys."

Leo lifted his head and touched his uncle's face. "I wasn't scared, Tio. You were protecting us."

Abigail reached for her son. "I'm glad Tio Joaquin was quick to protect you. Are you ready to go to Tres Amigos for the soup jar party?"

He was all grins. "Yes!"

Oscar didn't look as confident. Lali held her hand out to him, and he moved to her. Luna stayed close to his side.

"Are you okay?" she asked in a low voice.

He nodded but stood in silence.

Lucas rubbed his hands together. "Joaquin, I'll drive your truck?"

Still looking rattled, Joaquin nodded and opened his truck door, giving Shadow and Luna the order to load up.

Oscar tightened his hold on Luna. "No."

Lali glanced around the churchyard. Most people had left. But still, she knew a public meltdown was the worst to recover from. "Can Luna go with us to the Tres Amigos?" *Please, please say yes.*

Lucas smiled and looked at Joaquin. "That works, right? I can drive and Luna can hang out with the boys?"

Joaquin nodded.

"Okay then. Let's go." Lucas opened the back door, offered her a hand and asked for permission to lift Oscar into the cab. Once they were settled in, Luna jumped in and lay across Oscar's lap.

Joaquin was sitting ramrod straight in the front seat with one arm around Shadow as he stared ahead.

She wanted to ask what had happened, but he didn't seem open to questions. Lucas hopped behind the wheel and started chatting about the sermon as if nothing was wrong.

Forcing herself to have a polite conversation with Lucas, she couldn't keep her gaze from moving back to Joaquin. Then she looked at her son.

He had draped himself over Luna and it didn't seem as if letting go was an option. She sighed. There were too many landmines for her to pick a path.

As if reading her mind, Joaquin twisted around and looked at her son, who was entangled with his dog.

"Since you're going to the Tres Amigos Ranch, you should keep Luna with you. You can drop her off at my place when you return to the cabin."

"Did I do something wrong?" Oscar spoke for the first time.

"No. It's me. I..." He paused, turned away and looked out the window. "I just need to figure some stuff out. It's better if I do it alone."

Wrapping her arms tighter around her middle, Lali suppressed the urge to reach out and hug him. Isolation swirled around him, even as he sat with other people.

Her instinct was to soothe him, but she was in no place to help someone else. Her life was a mess, and she needed to focus on her son. She ran her hand through Oscar's hair. He leaned away from her just a little, but she noticed, so she put her hands back in her lap.

There were so many people in her life who needed something that she couldn't give. She wanted to help but didn't know how. Her chest tightened. The urge to cry was ridiculous but nevertheless strong.

But she was stronger. She had to be. It was just all the upheaval that had made her so emotional.

Chapter Seven

Joaquin hated feeling out of control and his worst fear had just happened. He'd lost track of reality in public.

His brother Lucas jumped from the driver's seat and rushed over to help Oscar and Lali out. Just the other day Abigail had been complaining about Joaquin's truck. He should install the step-down like Lucas had. It would be more comfortable for his passengers. Why did everything about him make things difficult for the people around him?

With his little episode earlier, Lali and Oscar were probably scared of him now too. It had been so long since he'd had a time-shift episode. His uneasy feelings with the doctor and her son being on the ranch had him edgy. Then the boom with the boys running to the cars that triggered it. He should make a trip to San Antonio to meet with his group. It had been a while. He didn't want to unravel now.

Shadow nudged him. "I'm good, boy."

The back door opened, and Joaquin focused on the landscape in front of him. He heard Lucas and Oscar talking. Lali's light laugh floated his way.

He needed to replay Oscar and Leo getting to the parking lot safely until it was a solid memory and not tangled with the other two boys who had been killed on his watch.

Shadow nudged him again. "I know. The memories are back on the surface. Thanks for checking." He took a moment to steady his breathing and slow his heart rate.

"Oscar!" Leo was waiting on the porch since they had arrived first. The old ranch house had been turned into the ranch's offices. Kingston stood behind the boy.

Swags of evergreen tied together with red-and-black-checkered bows hung on every post. Icicle lights were already draped along the roof edge. On the porch a tall pine stood, ready for decoration. Or maybe they were going to leave it plain with the fake snow sprayed on it.

His outgoing nephew took a deep breath and slowed his pace as he approached Oscar. Kingston knelt in front of the boys and spoke to them. Oscar turned, looking back at his mother.

Lali was leaning against his truck. She nodded and Kingston led the boys and dog into the house. Lucas paused. There was a conversation too low for him to make out, then Lucas left too. Lali didn't move. Was she waiting for him?

He had planned to just wait it out in his truck or walk home. If he cut straight across the pasture, it wasn't far. She didn't move. It was getting colder by the minute. Why wasn't she going inside with the others?

A gust of wind ruffled her hair. The loose waves didn't quite touch her shoulders and her sweater offered no warmth. He grabbed his jacket from the middle console and opened his door.

"Here. It's getting cold." He handed her the jacket that used to be his father's favorite. It was vintage leather with a comfortable fleece lining. It would swallow her, but it was better than that thin sweater she had now.

"Thank you." She slipped it on and snuggled in it. "This is so comfy. Are you sure you don't need it?"

"I'm good. I tend to run hot." Seeing her in his dad's jacket did funny things to his heart, and right now with his brain chemistry being unstable, he didn't need any more struggle. "You should go in. Oscar might be looking for you."

"I told Lucas to come get me if he gets agitated." She took in the festive house with a smile. "Before today I wouldn't have believed that Oscar would ever go inside a place without me. Especially a new place with strangers. It's because of you and Luna. It never occurred to me that a dog could change his life and give him independence."

"Luna and Oscar click in a way I wouldn't have expected. This is why I work with these dogs. They change people's lives."

"Did Shadow do that for you?" She nodded to his companion that stood close to him, on guard for another misstep.

"He did." He stroked Shadow's head. "Today was the first time in about two years that reality shifted for me. But he was able to pull me back in seconds. I'm so sorry. I didn't mean to scare the boys."

"I know. Are you okay? That has to be traumatic to lose your sense of time and space."

He raised his gaze to meet her. Most people didn't really get it, but she did without him even explaining it. "It is. I just need a little time to…" He took a deep breath. "To recalibrate and plant the memory of the boys being happy and safe as they get in the car to leave. No tragedy. Just a trip to the neighbor's ranch."

She moved closer and put a hand on his sleeve. The cuff of his jacket covered her long slender fingers. He could just see the tips of her short nails. The glossy pink paint seemed out of place on her. It was chipped in a few places from the cave. They were probably done for her wedding.

His stomach twisted. Just the other day she was on the brink of saying *I do* to another man.

"You knew some boys who didn't get safely into their car?" Tears were in her large brown eyes, making them shine.

He shouldn't have said anything about that. His memories would ruin her day. "We should go inside." Pulling away from her would be the right thing to do, but the warmth of her touch kept him still.

"If you want to talk about it you can." She moved closer and wrapped her arm around his. "I'm sorry. A stranger who popped up in the middle of the night is probably the last person you want to talk to. You just really helped me yesterday from feeling completely alone and I want to offer you the same comfort. I get it if it's too difficult."

She looked at the house. "Should we both go inside? You shouldn't be out here alone. I find being nosy about something else, like secret caves or someone else's problems, can help me get my mind out of my own problems. Not that there is anything in my life that compares to what you've gone through. I just mean…" She sighed. "Sorry about the rambling. I'll stop talking now."

The corner of his mouth quirked up and a dry laugh found its way out of his chest, knocking a few cobwebs out of the way. It had been a while since he'd wanted to laugh. "Sometimes it's easier to talk to a stranger." He wanted to talk. But it wouldn't be fair to her.

"You know the interesting thing about the way I grew up?" Lali said. "I've been to places in the world most people haven't even heard of. In developing countries I've been exposed to things most people can't imagine happening in our world. The way women and children are treated. Things that are done for statues and political power. For the most part, people in developed countries take the feeling of safety for granted." She sighed. "So, if you're worried about shocking me, I have a few stores of my own. The world is a dangerous place and pockets of it don't value human life the way we're taught."

He nodded. "We were in Isreal as a training exercise. No combat. Nothing dangerous. One day my group went out to watch procedures at a checkpoint. I met these two boys." He paused. "About Oscar and Leo's age. They were practicing their English with me. They were joking around and laughing. Their mom kept telling them to settle down and then I would wink at them. That just caused them to giggle more." He made sure to take a minute and picture the boys and their smiling faces. They were not Oscar and Leo.

"The car pulled away, and farther down the

road there was an explosion. One of the boys survived and when I tried to get through, I was blocked. I tried to find him, and I was told he had an uncle that took responsibility. I wasn't allowed to contact him to make sure he was okay. There was no follow-up."

The wind pushed the trees around and some acorns fell. "Today when the boys were laughing and going to the cars, I heard an explosion, and I was turned upside down. I had to protect the boys. Mentally, I shifted so fast Shadow didn't have time to prevent it."

They stood in silence for a while, the wind having a conversation with the trees. He closed his eyes to ground himself here, in Texas Hill country. The land of his ancestors.

She stepped closer, her warmth soothing him in a way he hadn't expected. Her voice was low and steady. "It must be awful to lose control of reality like that. Our brains are so powerful." Her side hug grew tighter, like she wasn't going to let him fall into the black pit of his subconscious. "But our boys are fine. They are inside listening to Christmas music and feeling loved."

"They are. That's what I need to map out in my mind. The brain can't always tell the difference between the past and present. Shadow helps me stay grounded."

They stood in silence as the wind danced

with the trees. Lali's presence anchored him. He shouldn't be this comfortable with her, but he couldn't bring himself to break contact.

His sister poked her face out the door and raised her brows at him. "Are y'all coming in? We've got Frito pie and Big Red floats."

Lali looked up at him. "I have no idea what either of those things are."

The pressure in Joaquin's chest dissipated. Lightness and ease rolled their way through his body. He could get used to this. "Well then, you're in for a treat." He stepped forward and her hand slipped off his arm and into his hand as he led her under the Christmas garland and into the house.

Lali hadn't even realized she still held his hand until Abigail's gaze darted between them, her eyes full of…something. Wonder? Disbelief? Skepticism?

The contact with him was so natural. Her heart rate picked up and she became uncomfortably warm. Too easy. Too fast.

At the same time, she didn't want to pull her hand away from Joaquin if the contact helped him in any way.

The room smelled like every Hallmark Christmas card she'd ever imagined would smell like if they were scented. Wild pine, apple, cinnamon and sugar tickled her nose.

"What is that delicious aroma?" she asked.

"Apple pies, gingerbread men and sugar cookies," Letti, Kingston's mother, said with pride. "This is our very first Christmas together as a family." She stood between Kingston and Naomi, arms interlocked. Abigail had explained that Kingston had grown up thinking Letti was his mother, only to discover recently that she was his aunt. His birth mother was Naomi, who he had been told was his cousin. That had to be unsettling. But they all seemed so close and happy.

"Thank you for including Oscar and me."

"We're happy you're here." Letti's big smile was contagious. "We've been so excited to be involved with the church programs this year. I want everything to be perfect."

Abigail rubbed her hands together. "It will be. This side is tortilla soup and five beans. Over here is chicken noodle and my favorite, Italian barley soup." She put everyone at a station. "Lali, can you pour the rice and pass it to Lucas?"

"Sure." It was exciting to be part of a community tradition.

Christmas music played in the living room and everyone started talking as they handed the jars down the line.

Oscar and Luna moved next to Joaquin. The

boy had his face down and his arm around Luna. He was singing a song under his breath. This was too much for him. Would Joaquin take them home if she asked? Surely everyone would understand.

Before she could leave her station, Joaquin was kneeling in front of Oscar, signing. Joaquin nodded to her and smiled, letting her know he had her son.

As the beans, rice, pasta, seasonings and spices were beautifully layered, Joaquin and Oscar moved to the edge of the busy kitchen and set up a station with boxes. Oscar sat in the hallway but could still see where Lali worked. He signed that he was going to help Joaquin.

After their packing corner was set up, Joaquin signed *Good job*. When her son smiled at him, she just about lost her heart.

"Dr. Kan," Lucas hollered across the room to get Lali's attention. "How did you become interested in Earth's history and caves? I didn't even know that was a job."

"I grew up in the academic world, mainly in the halls of the Universidad Nacional Autonoma de Mexico in Mexico City. My mom has her doctorate in earth science engineering and my father is very passionate about his studies in Aztec history and linking it to the present."

"How did you meet Isaac?" Abigail asked.

"My parents were doing research and taught at A&M so I decided to do my doctorate. We were in a class together studying DNA. Within those strands the history of our past is linked to our future."

"No wonder you and Joaquin get along so well." Abigail elbowed Lucas and they both smirked at their big brother. It looked as if he growled at them.

"He loves to tell us that saving the past is the best way to protect the future," Lucas chuckled.

Isaac nodded, paying more attention than it seemed. "He worked with ranchers in Mexico to build a herd of longhorns based on the DNA of the original herd that were able to survive. He's done the same with a small herd of mustangs."

"He says the horses weren't new but were re-introduced to this part of the world." Leo looked very proud of his uncle. "Tito says he's the best cowboy out of the lot."

"I don't know about that." Lucas sounded very offended. "Don't forget the native grasses. Don't get him started on the importance of reestablishing those."

"Really?" She turned to Joaquin. She'd had no clue his interest ran that deep. "Which university programs are you working with?"

Lucas laughed. "The school of hard knocks. He hates education. Think it's a waste of time."

"I don't hate it." Joaquin glared at his grinning brother. "I spend a lot of time online reading reputable sites and whatever. The most important part is listening to the old-timers in the mountains of Mexico. They're connected to the original tribes that've survived in the wildest part of the territory. They're a valuable source of information. More so than modern buildings with all their high tech."

She added rice to more jars but didn't break eye contact. "And the best researchers spend time collecting those stories and using their top-of-the-line technology to record, analyze and document what they find. Then they write the articles you read online. When I was ten, we spent almost two years in the mountains of Peru doing just that. That's where I discovered my love for caves and hidden history. My parents weren't happy with my new passion."

"Some of us here are not happy at the thought of opening our land to the public," Joaquin stated.

The jar filling stopped and everyone went silent.

Joaquin dropped his gaze to the jars he was putting in the dividers. "Sorry. Abigail, you should know better than to include me in public events."

Letti chuckled. "No biggie. We all know how you feel about the cave. How about we practice the songs we have picked for caroling?" She put the last of her noodles in a jar and passed it to Joaquin with a smile.

Lali bit her lip. Why had she gotten defensive and short with him? This was supposed to be a fun activity. "I love Christmas music."

Abigail nodded. "We'll sing one song at each house. Some ask for another and want to talk a bit. The visit is just as important as the gift. So having three good songs would be perfect."

"Have you caroled before?" Naomi asked Lali.

"I have. We spent one Christmas in London, and I got to sing with the music department when I was sixteen. But Oscar has never really been around any traditional Christmas events."

"Wow. We aren't that fancy." Abigail's eyes were wide.

"Oh, it's not about being fancy. It's about sharing the love and joy of the holidays. I want that for Oscar. I appreciate that you've included us." She avoided eye contact with the man working with her son.

Life on the ranch, with this family, was so different from life with her parents. But her appearance apparently wasn't wanted by everyone. She thought she and Joaquin had connected outside, but it had to be all in her head. She wasn't good at reading personal situations and Joaquin had her confused.

Not that it mattered. She was here to put an end to her parents' plans for her and to explore an uncharted cave. This was a new beginning for her and Oscar. It was better if it wasn't complicated by a man.

"Joy to the World" came on and Letti cast her phone to the TV screen that hung on the kitchen wall. Lali's heart became lighter as her voice joined the others. Oscar listened and studied the screen. The third time they sang it he joined in.

Joaquin sealed the jars but kept his head down. His mouth stayed closed.

Why was he such a jerk? Joaquin focused on sealing the jars and stacking them. When the first container was full, he moved it to the side and prepared the second one.

This was why he worked with animals and plants. People were complicated and he didn't respond the way he should. Right before he and Lali came into the house she had been so understanding, and he had allowed her to ground him. Now he was acting as if she was the enemy. That had to be totally confusing for her.

Everyone started singing. It was one of his mother's favorite Christmas songs. She'd loved Christmas, and growing up they had all been in the church choir. Music had been part of their daily lives, with worship music always playing in their home.

He was happy that Abigail and his brothers were able to reconnect to that joy, but he couldn't—it was too painful. The last jar was passed to him, and he sealed it.

"Thanks. I'm going to walk back to the house."

"You're not going to sing with us?" his sister asked, her hands on Leo's shoulders. "I was hoping you'd stay."

She looked so disappointed. He was used to that look. It eventually found its way to everyone he loved. "It's been a day, and I need to check on the yearlings."

"Wait." Lali ran to the pile of coats. "Here. It's gotten colder. If you're walking, you need this. Thanks for letting me borrow it. What about Luna?"

He took the coat. His gaze went to the end of the counter where Luna sat between Kingston and Oscar. The boy's hand was casually resting on her. "Lucas can bring her when he drops off my truck."

Then he turned and headed out into the cold. If he lingered any longer, he'd find an excuse to stay. Carefully closing the door behind him, he paused for a moment and listened to "O Come, All Ye Faithful." Was he trusting God and following Him or was he running and hiding?

Images of Celeste and Ethan in the kitchen making gingerbread men for Christmas made an unwelcome appearance.

It had taken a good bit of time for her to convince him it was safe to love her and her son. And he had finally opened his heart for them.

For the first time since he was seventeen, hope had him believing in a family of his own. Then with just one visit from her ex she dropped him, cutting all ties.

How many times could he put himself out there only to lose everything he held dear?

Chapter Eight

It had only been two weeks since Lali had driven into his life. For the most part he'd been able to keep everything very professional with her and Oscar. Luna and Oscar had been working well together. A couple of times he'd gone into the cave with Lali. That had almost been too much, seeing her at work.

Now he was in the last place he should be. At the church, he pulled into an empty parking spot next to his family's SUV. His hand paused on his truck key. *What am I doing?*

Joaquin let out a puff of air. Was he looking for trouble? Tonight was about spreading Christmas cheer and goodwill. He was the last person who should be here.

Members of his family and the Zayases would be going door to door singing and passing out the soup jars they had made. That fact alone was God in action. A year ago, it couldn't have happened.

The two families had been adversaries, believing the worst of each other. But then his little sister had fallen in love. Love and hope could change everything when God was in control.

Giving up control was tough for him. It was too risky.

Luna made a soft whimper. He glanced into the back seat and looked at the two dogs. Shadow was watching him. Luna had her nose pressed to the window.

It had been a week since they had seen Lali or Oscar. Luna had been pouting. He pushed out any thoughts that pointed to him being unsettled too. Oscar needed Luna tonight.

Christmas caroling. It shouldn't be this hard. His mother would want him to do this.

"Boy I haven't done this since…" His throat cut off the words but his brain didn't take the hint. It plowed ahead with memories he had blocked since he was seventeen. Shadow laid his chin on Joaquin's shoulder and gently pressed his cool nose against his neck. Then the dog sat back and looked at him.

Cutting eye contact from Shadow, Joaquin looked at the church. The tall, twisted oaks were covered in gold lights. Bright green wreaths with red ribbons hung on the door and over each window. The youth building was even more festive: silver bells, stars and giant shimmering balls woven together with red ribbon and evergreens.

Each column was covered, and more garland

was draped across the porch roof, highlighted with colorful lights. A wooden Nativity scene that he had helped build during middle school was still placed in front of the large windows.

Inside, everyone was being divided into groups, and Letti and Abigail were passing out sheet music, organizing the soup jars and marking the homes they would be singing at.

It was a tradition going back to before he was born. And there had not been a Christmas he had missed until the accident. Had it really been over twenty-five years ago? A whole lifetime without them.

In the first year, his grandfather had shut them in the house. Life outside of their ranch had stopped. The core of their family was gone, and shock lingered. None of them had complained about not participating in the community. They had shut down. But the twins, Abigail and Isaac, had been too young.

That year, the carolers had come to *their* door for the first time ever. Tito and Lucas had hidden in the barn, leaving Cyrus and Joaquin standing there with forced smiles, and Abigail cheering in delight. He blinked—where had Isaac been? Probably hiding in the closet that he had turned into his secret room.

They had been given soup jars and sad smiles before being left alone. Those now-empty jars were probably still buried in the back of the pantry.

He knew the church body had meant well, but it had been too soon for them. Abigail had rejoined the caroling sometime in middle or high school. Joaquin had been gone by then.

Since she had returned home with Leo, she'd jumped right back in. She was probably chair of the committee now. His baby sister believed in the healing power of the season and reaching out to those in need.

Luna whined as if she knew her favorite person was just yards away. Not allowing his brain to add any more doubt to his decision, he turned off the engine. "I'm going. Cool your jets."

The door to the youth building opened and out came a herd of laughing carolers. The variety of people had one thing in common. They looked like they had stepped out of a Victorian Christmas card. The cool weather had the women in velvet cloaks lined with fake fur. Some of the men wore top hats and long coats.

Shoulders above the crowd was Kingston. He was right by Abigail's side, looking as happy as everyone else to be part of this chaos. Joaquin's future brother-in-law was missing the fancy hat, but he had a red scarf tied around his neck and a long black coat.

Abigail spotted Joaquin sitting in his truck and

paused. Confusion marred her features. With a tilt of her head, she narrowed her eyes as if doubting what she saw. Lucas came up behind her and laughed. Literally—he threw his head back and laughed out loud then waved. Something was seriously wrong with that boy.

Sure he was glaring, Joaquin relaxed his features. It was good for him to be unpredictable.

His father's jacket and black cowboy hat were going to have to do. Grabbing his guitar, he stepped out of his truck. Shadow jumped down and sat next to him, pressing his body against his leg.

One group of joyful carolers hurried past him and waved, wishing him a Merry Christmas on their way to their cars. A few gave him a strange look, but most were just excited about the night in front of them.

He opened the back door. Luna waited for permission and then joined Shadow once he gave them the sign. She hummed with excitement but stayed in place. He had taken the time to wrap their collars in fake holly, with a red bow tie for Shadow. If he had planned ahead, he could have gotten them that reindeer headgear. The boys would have loved that. Maybe next year.

Oscar and Leo came running. Leo laughed. "Oscar said you were coming with Luna, but I told him you'd never come. You don't like people."

"I like people just fine." He ruffled his nephew's hair. "But Luna loves people, especially Oscar. She thought he might need some extra support tonight."

"She's talking to you again." Then Leo's eyes went wide. "You brought your guitar! You're going to sing with us?"

"That's the plan."

Another group of Dickensian carolers came right toward him, like they wanted to talk. The urge to flee made his legs antsy, but Shadow brushed up against him. Burying his fingers in the soft fur, he held his ground.

Most of the jolly makers waved to him and kept walking. A few stopped and greeted him. Cindy, an old family friend, hugged him and said how proud his mother would be.

That's what he didn't want to hear. His jaw clenched at the thought that he had disappointed her with his life choices.

With a few pats on the back, they moved on quickly. Everyone had their assignments. They were piling into the lineup of SUVs and heading out. There looked to be five groups of goodwill ambassadors.

Now a small group surrounded him, mainly his family. Lucas was his only brother there, and he wore a top hat with a sprig of holly tucked into the band. He raised an eyebrow at his younger brother.

With a grin, Joaquin shrugged. "Abigail loves this, and it makes her happy."

Where would they be if they had lost her too? They'd be a much sadder lot of humans than they were now, that's for sure.

"You just holding that to look pretty, or are you really going to play?" Abigail asked.

"I figured it would be a good activity for Luna, and if Oscar was here, he could use the company." He slung the guitar strap over his shoulder and patted Shadow.

Lali was standing on the other side of his brother. No need to make make eye contact. He was here for Luna and Oscar.

Lali had her hand over her heart. "The guitar is my favorite instrument."

His stupid heart jumped in pride.

Abigail hugged him a little longer and tighter than normal. "I'm so glad you are here." She was on the edge of tears.

"Hey. None of that. Tonight is supposed to be fun." He hugged her back.

"Emma's on her way. Something happened at the ranch that delayed her."

On cue, one of the ranch trucks pulled into the parking lot. His niece launched out of the back seat and waved with a huge grin on her face. "I have an early wedding gift for you!"

In unison, all three doors opened, and his brother Cyrus, along with their grandfather, got out, both dressed as Victorian gentlemen. Isaac stepped out from the back. He was in his normal white starched shirt and jeans. A cluster of holly berry leaves tied together with red string was tucked into his black cowboy hat band.

Now full-on crying, his sister ran to them and pulled them into one giant hug.

Lali moved closer to Joaquin. "She's very excited. I take it this is a big event. Maybe Oscar and I shouldn't be intruding on a family moment."

"It's been a while since we've done this as a family. Not since Abigail was three. You don't get to leave now." His voice sounded raw to his own ears. "Once my sister claims you, you're part of the family."

She blinked a couple of times. *No, no, no.* "Hey, no tears. I know we're frightening, but I promise we're harmless. If you want to leave at any time let me know."

With a deep breath, she seemed to get herself under control.

He looked over Lali and watched his sister lead his oldest brother, his younger brother and his grandfather to the group. His throat burned, holding back years of memories. "We haven't done this as a family since the accident."

Shadow stood on his hind legs and gently put his paw on Joaquin's chest. He ruffled the dog behind his ears and pressed his forehead to his. "Thank you, boy."

Emma literally jumped her way to the rest of the family. She told Lucas how handsome he looked in his hat and hugged Kingston and his mothers. She ruffled Leo's hair and then saw Joaquin.

She tilted her head as her eyes grew shiny. "Tio Joaquin. You're here too. This is truly the perfect night that Tia Abigail and I prayed for." Then she hugged him as if she never wanted to let him go.

How was he supposed to find peace when everyone could be lost in the blink of an eye? How could he truly trust God to keep everyone safe, when there was already so much loss?

His niece went to Abigail, and they sorted everyone into two Suburbans. He was assigned the back seat with Lali and Oscar so the dogs could ride behind them.

"This must be exciting to have everyone in one place." Lali's smile had an edge of uncertainty to it.

"I'm happy for Abigail. This is a true gift for her."

"But it's too much for you?"

He looked out the window. Warm yellows, reds and pinks highlighted the hills as the sun disappeared behind the horizon. "It's just a lot of painful memories also. But Abigail is working to make new ones." He wanted to talk about anything but the emotion this little trip stirred up. "What about you? Any long-standing family traditions?"

"No. We were always just observing others' traditions, not really a part of them. All the different experiences were great, but no real roots for my family. I didn't really know my grandparents, and I couldn't tell you anything about my great-grandparents on my mother's side. My father's lineage is all about bloodlines and ancestral history. No personal traditions. My parents really don't celebrate Christmas."

"I haven't in a while either. I'm usually gone."

"For twenty-five years?" The question was soft, not accusatory.

"Yeah. Looks like I'm going to be breaking a twenty-four-year streak." His gut was in knots. It was so much easier to just be busy somewhere else and not have to think about it.

With Lali and Oscar, it seemed even more dangerous to hang around.

Lali wanted to ask more questions. She wanted to dig deeper into the reasons this man avoided his wonderful family. It was clear he loved them.

He loved the ranch. So why keep a distance between them?

Being in the car with Abigail and Kingston meant the conversation was all about their wedding. Since she had nothing to contribute, and Joaquin had shut down, she settled back and started making a mental list of what she needed for the cave.

"You're coming, right?" Abigail asked from the front.

Lali had no idea what she was talking about. She blinked, trying to sort out possible answers.

"The wedding," Joaquin offered. "You can tell her no." He said it low enough that no one else would hear him.

"You have to come. You're part of the family now," Abigail went on without giving her a chance to respond.

"Maybe she..." Joaquin started, but Lali put a hand on his arm.

"I'd be honored," she said loudly.

The thought of going to any wedding had her stomach in knots, but Abigail had been so welcoming. She leaned in and whispered back to Joaquin. "It would be rude to stay in the cabin." The smell of woodland and leather had her fighting to remember why she was this close to him.

"I wouldn't think a wedding would be the place you want to be anytime soon."

"Just because I had a disastrous day doesn't mean I hate all weddings. They seem so in love. It'll be good for me to see this."

He quirked his mouth and raised one brow, making his skepticism very clear.

"First stop the Dryers' place." They drove down a long dirt road and Kingston stopped the truck.

Abigail shared a brief family history, then they all got out. Cyrus had parked behind them, and they all formed a small, two-tier semicircle around the front steps. Abigail went to knock but paused as she looked at them. "Thank you, each and every one of you, for being here with me. I've dreamed of the day."

Cyrus coughed. "Knock on the door. If you keep this up, we'll never get home in time to decorate the tree."

Her eyes went wide. "We have a tree at the house?"

Emma clapped. "That's why we were late."

The door behind Abigail opened and an older woman who had looked exhausted now lit up with a smile. "Oh, you're my carolers!" She went to hug Abigail. "I came to your place when you had just lost your sweet grandma and mother, and now you're here at my house. What a blessing. Let me get Hank." She hurried back into the house and while she was gone Joaquin warmed up his guitar.

He stood a little off to the side, separate from the rest of them. But the music wrapped around them and pulled them all closer. It was beautiful and soft. So unexpected from the large mountain man.

Abigail joined Lali, so she quickly averted her eyes from Joaquin to the front door.

"I find it very interesting, his sudden interest in social engagements," Abigail said. She looked across at her big brother.ABigail said. She looked bottom lashes. "He seems to be melting into the boy Cyrus told me he used to be, before the accident, then the military and, well, other events of this world that made an ice wall around his heart. I don't know what's going on. I'm happy but also worried. Be careful with my big brother. I fear he's easily broken."

The door opened and the Dryers greeted them.

The DeLeon family was unexpected for Lali. She had needed a place to get her footing and God had provided. This was a family that loved and supported each other even when they disagreed.

As a group they sang "Joy to the World." Oscar had his eyes closed and his mouth stayed shut but he was swaying to the song, with one hand loosely stroking Luna. He was relaxed and enjoying the evening. Her eyes burned with tears.

This was the kind of environment she wanted

to raise her son in, not the competitive academic world. But her work and her life were in that world. How could she change course now?

Chapter Nine

By the last house Joaquin was exhausted, but on the other hand spending time with his family had been better than he thought. There had been so much more laughter than sadness. Had he been hanging on to loss so tightly over the years he had let joy slip by?

When they were back at the church he'd offered Lali and Oscar a ride because of Luna. Now he was alone in his truck with them. Not the smartest choice.

Oscar bounced in his seat. "They said they have a real Christmas tree they cut down on the ranch. It's a Texas piñon pine. *Pinus remota*. They're common north of here in Edwards Plateau but you have a special cluster around the opening of your cave facing north. The young ones have the perfect cone shape for a classic Christmas tree. But they can get up to thirty feet. They live up to a thousand years. They've been around since the Pleistocene Era. And the thin-walled seeds are a highly desirable food source for wildlife and the Indigenous people of this region. Leo said I can help decorate it. Can we help, Momma?"

She grinned. "How can I say no? Especially after spending an evening singing Christmas songs. What better way to finish off the evening than decorating a Christmas tree?"

"Leo told me they have family ornaments, and he's made some of them too. Do we have family ornaments? I don't remember making ornaments. Is ornament making a tradition that we should have? Traditions are good. Abuelita says traditions are what keep history alive."

"We have not been in one place long enough to collect Christmas decorations. Maybe next year we'll have our own place."

"But isn't the lodge our home now? Why can't we decorate it? It's our place."

Lali looked a little frazzled. "I..."

She didn't seem to know what she was going to say. After a few minutes of silence, Joaquin decided to jump in. "If you want a tree, we can go tomorrow and cut one down. I know exactly where they are. So, while your mom is poking around in the cave, we can have the tree at your house before lunch. And if I know my sister, she has extra decorations. Growing up, we made a lot of our decorations."

"How?"

He shrugged. "Paper chains, glitter, string, dried fruit and sometimes dough with cinnamon sprinkled in them so they smelled good. Tita and Mom were very crafty."

Oscar clapped. "I can research Mexican traditions. That would make Abuelita and Abuelito happy." He yawned. Then he shut his eyes and slumped.

"Oscar? Are you okay?" There was worry threaded in Lali's voice.

The boy popped his eyes open. "Can we get a tree without cutting one down? *Pinus remota* are important to a diverse biosystem. They grow slowly and live for a long time so they can provide homes and food for wildlife. You said you're returning the ranch to its original biodiversity ecosystem, so we shouldn't cut down a tree before its prime." He wiggled in the back seat. Luna put a paw on his leg. "The old ones are too big."

His breathing grew heavy and he hit his palms against his ears. "It's not the responsible thing to do. One was already cut down so we can't cut down another. We can't have a tree." His excitement about having a Christmas tree plunged into despair and his chest heaved in sobs.

Joaquin felt as helpless as the early days when Isaac would have a sudden meltdown. He looked at Lali to follow her lead. Tonight's activities had caught up to them.

"Oscar." She took his hands in hers. "Let's do the praying mantis and count." With their fingers pressed against each other in a prayer formation she counted. "Five. In. Four. Out. Three. In. Two. Out. One. In. Release." She repeated it until he was doing it with her.

His sniffles were softer as he dropped his hands and hugged Luna.

"Hey, partner." Joaquin kept his voice low. Oscar was overstimulated. "We won't cut down another tree. We can trim them and use the branches to make a tree on the wall. There are a million ways to decorate for Christmas without cutting down a tree. You could probably do some research with your mom and pick the best ones."

He was also formulating another plan, but he'd have to get his brothers involved.

"That sounds good." Lali looked at him with gratitude. "See? If we stay calm, we can think of other solutions."

Not lifting his head from Luna, the boy nodded, a few intakes of breath wavering from lingering sniffles.

Lali sighed. "It's been a very long night. Maybe we should go back to our cabin. We can get ready for bed and snuggle in to do research."

"Leo." The one word sounded so sad on Oscar's lips.

"It's okay, sweetheart. I'm sure he'll understand. Some people just need more space for downtime."

"Amen." Joaquin backed her up. He was all in for skipping the festivities and heading home. "Going to my cabin and enjoying the peace and quiet sounds perfect right now."

He sat up. "I'm better, Mom. Please. Leo is my friend. I want to see his tree. Please. I'm sorry I got upset."

Joaquin could see the war inside Lali. "How about we go for forty-five minutes?" he suggested. "We'll have Shadow and Luna. If we need to leave all we say is, *Luna's tired*. Any of us can say it and the others will not hesitate to leave. Deal?"

Relief flooded her eyes, and her shoulders relaxed. "Great plan. We can blame Luna. She's fine with taking the fall."

Oscar grinned.

Joaquin felt like a hero. Which was very dangerous. It was an addiction for him, and it had gotten him into trouble before. Being the hero never worked out long term and he just ended up letting people down.

It was time to make his plans for Mexico. The ranchers needed a temporary hero. He could do that.

Abigail was surprised to see everyone had arrived at the house. Even Isaac. He was carefully wrapping the staircase with green garland woven with red ribbon trimmed in gold.

The living room and kitchen were full of laughter and Christmas music. Boxes of decorations lay open around the room.

Abigail clapped when she saw them. Joaquin put his hand up. "We are only staying for a little bit. It's been a very stimulating evening."

She pressed her hands together and touched her chin. "I understand. I'm so grateful you came." Emotions made her voice wobble. "Do you know how long I've wanted this? And in a few days, I'm getting married. This is the last Christmas I'll be living under this roof. And everyone is here."

He pointed at her, his stare firm. "No tears."

"Right." She turned to Lali and hugged her. "I really think I have you to thank for this. It's the best prewedding I could have hoped for. Leo said he invited Oscar to decorate the tree."

"That's what I hear."

Luna and Oscar had already joined Leo, who was pulling a string of wooden cranberries out of a box. Joaquin made his way to the boys and started helping them drape the tree.

Abigail wrapped her arm through Lali's. "I had a lot of big Christmas wishes this year and you might be the best one I didn't even know I needed. Lucas and Kingston are helping me on the front porch. Do you have the tree under control?"

"I think so."

"Great. And no pressure. Whenever you need to leave just head out the door. We want good memories to be the lasting ones, and I know unrealistic expectations can tear them all down. So have fun and head out when it's time."

"Thank you." Why did it feel like she had known Abigail for years instead of weeks?

"De nada." She moved to the door then paused. "I know you're just here for the cave, but I feel you're connected to us in more ways than research. If you need anything, please don't hesitate. If nothing else, Isaac doesn't make many friends and that he counts you as one of them means a lot to me. So, no stress. Sorry if this is weird. I just was moved to tell you that." She gave her another smile, a slow, sweet one that held so much warmth.

No expectations. At any time in her life had she been free of high expectations? Her parents had had them for her before she was born. At first, she loved being with Avery because it appeared their relationship was free of expectations, but it turned out it had just been another type. He wanted to keep the party going all day every day. Which meant she was expected to take care of the messy daily life stuff like cleaning and paying the bills. He didn't want to live on a budget but expected her find a way to keep his credit flowing. With Matias it was about building his career and expanding his research. Everyone expected her to fall in line with their needs and goals.

She looked around the room. Emma had joined Joaquin and the boys. She was telling them a story that had the boys enthralled. Joaquin almost had a smile on his lips.

Rigo, their grandfather, and Cyrus were hanging garlands around the archway that led into the kitchen. Abigail was with Letti and Naomi setting up a collection of Nativity scenes on the huge mantel over the rock fireplace.

This was a home of love. Maybe some of the key players had been taken too soon, but they had held together. Why did Joaquin want to run from this?

With the warmth of the season and the love of the DeLeon family surrounding her, she went to the tree. "The lights and cranberries look good. What goes on next?"

"Mom, did you know they make strings of real berries and fruits and hang them in the trees outside for hungry wildlife? Can you do that at our home?"

Their home. He didn't seem to realize it wouldn't be theirs for long. They were just borrowing the hunting lodge. Soon they would be back on the campus with her parents. Working on research and fighting for grants. But they were here now, so she'd make the best of it.

"I like the idea of that. With the cold it's harder for wildlife to find food. What's next for this tree?"

Emma sat on the floor next to a box. "Next is all the embarrassing—"

Joaquin nudged her. "Don't be such a teenager." His niece received one of his rare smiles.

"Oh, I mean precious ornaments we've made over the years. Starting with baby handprints making angel wings." She pulled out a pair of laminated cutouts with ribbon tied on the top. "Look. It's my dad's and Tio Joaquin's little bitty baby feet. And here is yours, Leo. Look how little and cute."

Oscar turned to her. "Mom, do I have an ornament made of my baby footprints?"

"No. But I do have a couple of pictures of you with reindeer in Alaska. I can print them and make those into ornaments."

They placed all the angels on the tree, then pulled out more mementos from Christmases past. Rigo and Cyrus joined them, going over the memory each ornament carried with it. Then they opened a box of candy canes made of dough.

Rigo took one out and held it up as if it was a crown jewel. "Abigail and Isaac helped make these. They were only three. It was the last Christmas we were all together."

Cyrus gave a low chuckle. "I remember Mom

telling me to make sure they didn't eat the dough. Isaac tried but spit it out because of the high amount of salt. Joaquin, I think you ended up making most of these with Abigail. She loved it. Mom always said you were the most artistic one of us." Without looking at his brother, he turned and placed a few of the candy canes on the tree.

Joaquin didn't join him. He rubbed his forehead and stared out the window. On the front porch, Lucas was laughing and Abigail looked annoyed. Her fiancé was biting his lips as if trying hard not to laugh.

"You know what?" Lali said loudly. "I think Luna and I are tired. I'm ready to go home."

He turned then and looked at her in surprise. Then nodded.

She went to her son, knee-deep in glittery garland. "Tell Leo good night and thank you for letting us help."

Oscar awkwardly waved and smiled. "Momma said Luna is tired. That means we must leave. Thank you for inviting me, Leo."

"Bye." Oscar's new friend gave him a quick hug then ran to his cousin and helped her hang stars on the tree.

Joaquin and Shadow led them to the back door and helped them into his truck. He drove up the hill in silence.

He was at her door as soon as she had her seat

belt off. She took the hand he offered as she carefully slid down to the ground. "Why do you and your brothers all have trucks that need ladders?"

"I think it goes back to our tree house days. The ladder controlled who we let in."

Her hand stayed in his longer than necessary. "Was it a no-girls-allowed kind of tree house?"

"Pretty much. Then Abigail came along and turned it into an all-pink dollhouse."

She laughed. "I imagine you all encouraged her."

A real smile creased his face. "We did. She might have been a touch spoiled." For a split second they held eye contact. She could get lost in the depth of his eyes.

Then just as quickly, he stepped back, letting her hand fall from his. "Good night, Dr. Xitlali." Her name rolled off his tongue. She liked the sound of it.

A fog clouded her thoughts. She should say something, if for no other reason than to keep him close. "Thank you so much for sharing your family with us."

"Not sure you should be thanking me for that." He opened the back door, then moved out of her way so she could help Oscar down.

She reached for her son's hand. "Tell Luna good night. She has to go home to her bed," she added before he could ask for her to stay with them.

"Good night, Luna. You are the best dog in the history of the world." He kissed the top of her head and crawled out.

"Lali." Joaquin stood at the front of his truck. "Thank you. I know you did that for me. I appreciate it."

She knew he loved his family, but he also seemed to have an allergy to too much happiness. "It can be a lot sometimes. Even when it comes from a place of love. Good night, Joaquin."

Holding her son's hand, she went to the front door. Joaquin stayed there until they were inside and had the lights on. Then he got in his truck and drove away.

She didn't think she had ever met anyone surrounded by so much love who still felt all alone. The urge to hold him close was not something she should give in to. She was here to survey the cave. She would be leaving.

Too many people had already left him. She didn't want to do anything that would add her to his list of regrets.

Chapter Ten

"Mom! Mom!" Oscar ran into her room and jumped on the bed. It had been a rough night. She had not been able to shut her brain off. So she was not ready for this energetic version of Oscar.

"There's a Bobcat in our front yard," he yelled in her face.

That woke her up. "A bobcat?" She reached for her phone. Without a thought she dialed Joaquin's number. Her heart pounded. "Did you just see it through the window? Stay inside." Could a bobcat break a window or door?

"The Bobcat has a tree in its big claws. With all its roots."

Now he wasn't making sense. He turned as if to run out of her room, but she caught his hand. "Stay here." She put the phone to her ear. The phone just kept ringing. "I'm calling Joaquin."

"But he's on the Bobcat."

She blinked. "What?" Was she awake or was this a guilt-induced stress dream?

"Come on. Come look. They have a perfect

Christmas tree, and they dug a big hole right in our front yard to plant it. It won't die." He pulled at her.

She threw her long coat over her T-shirt and pajama bottoms and followed him to the living room.

"Look!"

He pointed out the front windows and sure enough, Joaquin was on some sort of white tractor with the word *Bobcat* written on the overhead bar. A huge three-shovel-looking claw was holding a ball of dirt that had a Christmas tree growing in it.

On the opposite side, Cyrus was sitting on a red mini backhoe. The scoop rested on a pile of freshly turned dirt and chunks of rock. Lucas and Isaac each had a bucket and poured something into the hole. Then they stood back. Joaquin moved forward, then stopped with the tree posed over the newly dug hole. He yelled something to his brothers, and Isaac made his way to their door.

"They're planting a piñon pine in our front yard." He tapped on the window and all the men turned. They waved when they saw him. Isaac knocked at the door.

Oscar ran to the door and flung it open, not even noticing the cold in his excitement.

"Is that a Christmas tree for me?" he asked.

"It is. Want to come help plant it?" Isaac was all grins.

"Yes. Yes."

He looked up at Lali. "Can he come outside?"

"Yes. She says yes." He turned from Isaac and ran to her. "Come on, Mom. Let's help them plant our Christmas tree. It's for us, right?"

"This is your Christmas tree," Joaquin yelled from the back of the running Bobcat. "Are you going to help us plant it?"

"Yes! Mom. Let's go!" He was jumping in place, his arms wrapped around his torso as his hands slapped his sides.

"Okay. But not until you get shoes and a coat on."

"Mom!"

Isaac turned and waved his hand to his brothers. "We'll wait until your mom says you can come out."

She followed Oscar to his room and found his shoes as he put on his coat. He was vibrating with happiness. "They're planting a Christmas tree in front of our house. We'll have it every year without cutting one down."

Lali swallowed back the tears at her son's happiness. There was no way she could tell him there wouldn't be a next year. Not here on the DeLeon ranch.

He ran from his room, and she put on her socks and boots without lacing them.

Oscar stopped at the door. "Mom." His voice was exasperated. "Let's go."

"I'm not going out there barefoot. Give me a minute. I'll be there. Go with Isaac if you want."

He didn't hesitate but spun around and left with the youngest DeLeon brother. Her heart gave a hard thump. Then she chuckled at her reaction. He had never been so fast to abandon her. That wouldn't have happened a month ago. He would anxiously wait for her before leaving the house. If they even left.

Isaac helped Oscar to climb into the Bobcat with Joaquin, and with his large hand guiding her son's small hands they lowered the tree into the hole.

Then Cyrus pushed the dirt back into the hole covering the roots. Lucas used a shovel to push the dirt down. Joaquin and Oscar put the Bobcat in reverse, then turned it off and joined Lucas and Isaac. They had a small shovel for Oscar. Surrounded by the largest men she had ever met, her small son helped them pack the dirt back around the roots and the trunk of the tree.

Cyrus loaded his tractor onto a flatbed she hadn't noticed earlier. How had they done all this before…? She checked the time on her phone. It wasn't even eight yet.

Lucas moved the Bobcat onto the flatbed, leaving Oscar with Joaquin and Isaac. They showed him how to stomp his feet to finish the packing.

Joaquin knelt in front of him and showed him something on the tree. It seemed to be a very serious conversation. Her son nodded and signed *thank you* as he said it.

Joaquin stood and called the dogs over. He released them and Oscar rolled around hugging them and burying himself in their thick fur.

Isaac greeted the dogs, then with a wave turned to the road and walked to his equine center. A cool breeze came across and caused Joaquin's hair to dance around his face. It needed a cut, but she was starting to like the wild-mountain-man look. Then he pushed it back and smiled at her. Her traitorous stomach took a dive.

Nope. None of that. She stayed on the edge of the deck. Keeping a safe distance would be smart.

He didn't allow her that space. While walking to her he gestured to the tree. "Merry Christmas! Every kid needs a tree. My best memories were lying flat on my back underneath ours with all the lights on." He stopped next to her, leaned on the railing and watched Oscar play with the dogs.

She remained silent, but he didn't seem to mind. They stood there while her son and his dogs roughhoused. For their size, the Akitas were incredibly gentle.

"I've never done that with a tree outside." He broke the silence first in a low, almost wistful-sounding voice. "I wonder if the sky makes it more magical or does all the openness take away from the sparkling lights?" After a long moment, he turned to her. "What was your favorite thing to do at Christmas as a kid?" So, he wasn't going to let her stay silent.

"I don't know. We spent a few years around Oaxaca, Mexico, and I fell in love with the nine days of posadas. I always wanted to be one of the kids running from house to house dressed as an angel. Are you familiar with the custom?"

"I am. The local village in the mountains where I've worked with the ranchers makes a big deal of the nine days leading to Christmas Eve. It represents the nine months of Mary's pregnancy, right? We don't do anything like that here. I do remember all the kids participating. They loved it. Why didn't you?"

"My parents are strong believers in being observers. Collect the data. I mean I wanted that candy, but I wasn't part of the community. The part I loved most was the villancicos."

"Villancicos?" He tilted his head. "I'm not sure I know that word. What is it?"

"While everyone follows the children going from house to house, they sing traditional Christmas carols. They called them villancicos."

"Oh, like caroling."

She laughed. "I guess so. I just realized your family let me live one of my childhood Christmas wishes. It was truly a gift. Just like this tree. We've never really had our own Christmas."

"You weren't even allowed to sing with them?"

"If you get too emotionally attached your observations can become biased. So, no."

From the corner of her eyes while she was trying not to look at him, she saw his frown. "Sorry. That's not what you meant when you asked about my best memory. It wasn't bad or anything. We were just always somewhere different. I don't have memories of personal family traditions. I did have the privilege of experiencing cultural traditions that most kids don't."

"You mean observing." He turned from her and watched Oscar for a bit. "What about with Oscar? Do y'all have any traditions or just something you did once that he remembers? In my experience, it doesn't take much for kids to think something is a tradition."

She tilted her head. "The one thing he has talked about nonstop is making the jars of soup. He's already talking about decorating this tree for next year. He's never talked about Christmas or plans for the future."

Oscar laughed as he ran in a big circle around the tree, the dogs in pursuit.

"You should ask Oscar instead of me. There might be a memory that's important to him that I didn't even notice. Most of the time he keeps his feelings to himself. He likes dealing with facts and deep research."

"Yeah, I've noticed." He chuckled as if it was not a problem at all. "Isaac was like that as a kid. Still is even though he tries to keep it to a minimum now. I think it's hard for him to try to remember social norms."

They fell into silence again.

"Well, I guess now I'll have to get some weather-safe ornaments."

"Oh man. I forgot." Joaquin darted toward his truck, then at the bottom of the steps turned back and looked at her as he walked. "I have solar lights. And I asked Abigail about decorations." He opened the back door to his truck cab and lifted two large bags into the air. "We have everything we need to make wildlife-friendly ornaments."

How could this man be real? And more importantly why was she working so hard not to notice him? Maybe because she showed up at his door in a wedding dress, and he was smart enough not to notice her?

She was a mess at personal relationships. Avery and Matias were all the proof anyone needed. Her son and the cave were all she should be focused on right now.

Joaquin took the bags to the porch. "Hey, Oscar. We have lights to put on the tree. Then we can string dried fruit and leaves for garland. I have peanut butter and birdseed for decorations." He looked inside the bag. "We have acorns and all sorts of stuff the animals can eat."

Oscar clapped and ran to the porch with the dogs on either side of him. "Deer should eat acorns, not corn." He dug into the bags and pulled items out.

Joaquin glanced at Lali and a bit of his joy from Oscar's excitement slipped away. Her arms were tight around her middle. *She didn't want him here*. What had he been thinking? All his brothers had left. He should have gone too.

He looked at his watch. "I have, um, things to check with the herd." Really, that was all he had? "Y'all have fun."

"No." Oscar ran to him. "You stay and help. Momma is too short to put the lights on. And the top of the tree needs something special. We can't reach it."

Lali gave him a sweet smile. "Oscar, he has other responsibilities."

Oscar frantically circled his flat hand over his chest then made a *Y* with his hands together and jerked them down. *Please stay*. Then he made the sign of *please* again.

Joaquin had been around Oscar enough to know he reverted to ASL when he was stressed. Dropping to one knee in front of the boy, Joaquin signed back that he would stay for a little bit. "I'll help with the lights. If it's okay with your mom."

"We would love for you to stay and help if you have the time." She kept her gaze on the tree.

Oscar pulled out the boxes of lights and signed, *Lights first.*

"I think there is a ladder in the back mudroom closet."

Oscar and the dogs stayed at Joaquin's side as he retrieved the giant A-frame ladder and placed it beside the tree, then climbed to the top. Lali reached up and handed him a string of lights. He zigzagged them through the branches as far as he could reach.

Oscar glowed with excitement as he helped guide the lights around the lower branches. "How will the lights work if we don't plug them in?"

"This is the solar panel. We'll plant it here beside the tree and when the sun goes down the lights will automatically turn on." He knelt at the foot of the tree and Oscar was right by his side. The dogs watched as intently as Oscar.

Joaquin covered the panel with his hand and the tree glowed with white lights.

Oscar gasped and signed the word *pretty.* Lali nodded in agreement. Joaquin's foolish heart swelled with pride, like he was the one who'd invented lights.

He removed his hand, and the lights shut off.

"Time to make the ornaments. Do you need help?" Any excuse to stay just a little longer.

"Yes." Oscar ran to the porch with Luna at his heels. Shadow nudged Joaquin as if sensing he needed a little extra care.

"Oscar can deal with a few nos. If not, he needs to learn." Her smile was so sweet and genuine.

"I'm good, if it's okay with you and I'm not intruding. It's been years since I made Christmas ornaments. It used to be an annual thing in our home, until... Well, until we lost our grandmother and parents. Even our uncle who had issues was at his best around Christmas." And in one moment they were all gone.

He closed his eyes. This was not the time. Oscar deserved happy Christmas memories. Just like the rest of his family.

Joaquin's heart tightened. He had thought the joys of Christmas had returned when he had Ethan. He was going to come home for the holidays to share his new family with the family he loved. Closing his eyes, he pushed all that false hope back into its box.

It was easier to avoid all the dark emotions that wanted to push up and consume him. Yes, he was protecting his heart, but at what cost?

Since Lali and Oscar had appeared on his doorstep, the Christmas cheer of his childhood had been rekindled and his heart was melting— maybe beating again.

He had the choice to run and hide or stay in place and let it burn. Through fire there could be rebirth.

Oscar lifted his hands. They were covered in peanut butter and seeds. Joaquin laughed as he tried to scrape them onto the empty paper rolls. "I think maybe we should have strung the dried fruit first. This is a mess."

Lali laughed as she tied off each cardboard column with large red paper bows. Her son giggled as the dogs licked the gooey mess off his hands. "Let's clean your hands so we can string the dried fruit," Lali said.

"It's going to be the most beautiful tree and the animals will love it. Right, Joaquin?"

"You speak the absolute truth, little man." Joaquin forced a smile.

Oscar gave him a real smile, full of love, and Joaquin knew at that moment without a doubt that it was too late to lose them without more damage to his heart.

The goal now was to minimize that injury.

The boy ran to the tree with a long line of fruit flying behind him. He stumbled and almost fell but kept going.

Lali put her hand over her chest. "He is so outgoing here on the ranch."

"Ranch life is good for kids. As much as we didn't understand what was going on with Isaac as a kid, being here, on the land with the animals, gave him enough freedom to be himself. That's probably what saved him when we didn't have a clue."

"I can see that." They joined Oscar, and in the next twenty minutes had all the decorations on the tree.

"I can't wait for Leo to see it." Pride burst from the little man.

Time slowed as they stood close to each other, studying the tree and the endless sky beyond. Joaquin could stay here forever and be happy. But happiness never lasted.

"I better go." He started for his truck, but Lali was coming up behind him, so he stopped and looked at her. "Thanks for including me. This has been fun."

"I can't thank you enough for—" she gestured to the tree "—all of this. It's truly amazing. You all had to be up at 4:00 a.m. to get this done."

"It was worth his reaction. It'll be here every year, part of the lodge's history. This cabin could become your family tradition. If you want to come back." Until she met someone who didn't want her to come back here. "You know, to follow up on the cave. I'm sure there's more to study than a few weeks can cover."

"That's so true. That cave could be a lifelong project. Especially when you won't allow me a team," she teased. "But seriously. Thank you for the tree. It means more to us than you can ever understand." She stepped in and hugged him.

For a moment he froze. Why was she hugging him? He took a deep breath and forced himself to relax. It didn't mean anything. It couldn't.

He closed his eyes and allowed himself to be wrapped in her warmth for a few seconds. If he... A familiar car coming up the hill interrupted his thoughts.

They separated and waited for Abigail to join them. "Don't y'all look cozy."

"I'm leaving," he snapped. "She was just thanking me for the tree."

His sister laughed. "Okay."

"Leo!" Oscar yelled. "Come look at my tree."

"Oh, that looks perfect." Abigail put her hand on her chest. "Big brother, did you hang those lights?"

"He did." Lali said it in a way that sounded as if she was proud of him.

"You need to get in touch with Kingston. I want a million and one lights at the site where we are getting married. So, you've been voluntold."

"Yes, ma'am." He saluted her then went to his truck. His sister started bombarding Lali with wedding ideas.

He paused. She seemed to forget Lali had just been involved in a worst-case-scenario wedding day. Should he intervene and rescue Lali from an overzealous bride?

Lali wrapped her arm around Abigail's, and they walked toward their sons.

That was a good reminder that she didn't need him. She did need family connections and people to support her in building the life she wanted for herself and her son. His family was good at that.

Yes. He would step back.

He had a good life without complications. In a few days his sister would be getting married, and he would head to the mountains of Mexico. People there needed him too, and it wouldn't hurt when he left them.

Chapter Eleven

Lali dug her hands deeper in her pockets to keep her fingers warm. Abigail and Kingston's wedding day had arrived and she had been asked to keep Leo out of trouble at the main house until it was time for him to dress. She smiled. The boys didn't feel the cold as they played outside with Luna.

Watching the boys was good. It kept her mind from looping her disastrous weddings. Thinking of Joaquin was harder to control. When she wasn't in the cave or analyzing data, her mind wanted to examine every aspect of the mountain cowboy.

Since the planting and decorating of the tree he had gone into hiding. Early in the mornings she had caught glimpses of him in the fields below the hunting lodge. At times he was on horseback, other times just walking. Once she had seen him with the boys walking alongside him.

The grass had been waist high on the boys and they'd had their hands out gently touching the tops of the seed stems. When she had asked Oscar about it at dinner, he'd gone into details on the importance of restoring native habitats and the cycles of life starting with the health of the dirt. Then he'd asked her about the dirt in the cave. It was the first time he had shown interest in her work.

Joaquin stepped through the front door and stopped when he saw her. "I wasn't expecting to see you."

"She's keeping me out of trouble," Leo offered. "Abuelita Naomi says Momma is high-strung today and we need to help her focus so she can marry Kingston without any problems."

"My mom was going to marry Mateo but there must have been a problem because we ran away," Oscar said. "That's why we're hiding out here."

Leo's eyes went wide with horror. "If we mess this up, they might not get married? I want them to get married."

Heat climbed up Lali's neck. She could imagine how red her face must be now. "Oscar, no. It's not the same, Leo. Mateo and I..." Lali cut a glance to Joaquin then to the boys. "We needed to have a big talk, but we waited till the wedding. It's not... Well, anyway." Both boys were staring at her. "Your mom and Kingston had the talk before today. There is nothing that will interfere with their wedding."

"This is true," Joaquin said. "Abigail and Kingston are golden. But I do need help loading a long list of stuff into the Suburban. Anyone here waiting to volunteer?"

Both boys raised their hands high in the air. "We do! We can help."

"Great." He gave them both jobs and winked at Lali as he followed them around the side of the house. He picked up a cooler from the porch. It should have taken two people and the muscles across his back bunched and flexed. It was like he was trying to impress her, but that was ridiculous.

She wasn't even on his radar. Wishful thinking on her part. With a sigh, she sat on a rocker.

"Hey."

She jumped and a small scream escaped her chest.

His deep voice and warm presence surrounded her. He placed a hand on her upper arm. "Sorry, didn't mean to scare you."

"All my fault. I was deep in thought." She turned. He was so close. Close enough that if she leaned just a little, they could…

She stopped breathing and held very still.

He stared into her eyes for a long moment, then cleared his throat. "Oscar and Leo want to help unload. Is it okay if they go with Isaac and Lucas?"

Still feeling unbalanced, she nodded. He gave a thumbs-up to the boys, then turned back to her.

"Today has to be difficult."

"It is." The truth was out before she could guard it. In the depth of his gray-green eyes, she only found compassion and understanding. Had he been through a similar situation?

He opened the door. "It's gotten colder. A cup of hot chocolate sounds good. Want one?"

Before she could answer, Abigail slammed open the front door.

"Where's Cyrus?" Her eyes darted around the yard. "Where's Leo? Why is everyone missing?"

"It's okay." Joaquin pulled her in and hugged her. "Leo and Oscar are with Lucas and Isaac. They are going to Tres Amigos. They'll be right back. Cyrus is already over there. What's wrong?"

"I can't find Tito. He agreed to meet me in my room." She looked at her phone. "Over thirty minutes ago, but he didn't show and he's not answering his phone. Have you seen him? Is he with the boys?" Joaquin took her phone and wrapped his arms around her.

"It's okay. I haven't seen him, but I'll find him and bring him to your room." He tightened his hug.

"What if something happened? What if I put too much stress on him and his heart or..." She started crying.

"He's a tough bird who has survived more than your wedding."

"But I'm marrying a Zayas. He..." Her sob cut off her words.

"I need you to take a deep breath and think about why this day is important. I'll find him. He probably went to do some chores and lost track of time. You know him. Ranch work doesn't take a day off."

She reached her hand out to Lali. "We have tea and fancy little sandwiches upstairs. Since my brothers have Leo and Oscar, you should join us girls for a pre-wedding snack."

"Abigail—" Joaquin started.

"It's okay." Lali loved that he was worried about her feelings. "Thank you. It sounds nice."

He studied her for a long moment then nodded. "I'll text you as soon as I find him."

Abigail pulled her up the stairs. "You must tell me what is going on between you and my brother. He is so... I don't know. Like the way Luna stares at your son just waiting for her next command. I've never seen him like this."

"You just have that new-bride haze where you see..." She was going to say *love*, but that felt so wrong. "You just see things that aren't there." Joaquin did not look at her like that. She would notice, right?

"I know what I see. I have to talk about something to stay calm and you and Joaquin make a great subject. Maybe you'll stay longer than planned?"

Her stomach knotted. There was no way she could trust her own judgment. Maybe she should talk to Abigail, but not today. Today was a real wedding for two people who loved and respected each other.

Sadness hit her hard. Even Lali's first wedding, which she had thought at the time was all about love, had turned out to be false. There had not been any respect, just a youthful rebellion that had felt good temporarily. She had never known the kind of relationship Abigail and Kingston shared.

It didn't take Joaquin long to find their grandfather. He was in the old tack room that had been converted into a cowboy lounge for lack of a better word. He sat at the old rickety table. During calving season, whoever was on duty would play cards and games up here. Joaquin sent Abigail a quick text saying that he had found him, and all was good.

But one look at the old cowboy and anyone would know that was a lie. And Joaquin was the worst at any sort of emotional comfort. The only time he had ever seen his grandfather break was the hour before their family funeral. They'd stood alone in front of four caskets. Caskets that would all be lowered into the ground.

His grandfather had had to say goodbye to his whole family. Without warning, they were all gone, leaving him with a handful of grandchildren who were confused and lost.

Joaquin had never seen the man he admired above all else, the man who had always been his larger-than-life hero, so broken. It had scared him as a seventeen-year-old kid. That was the day Joaquin had started running.

First the army. But that had not been enough to escape the deep grief the people he loved were going through. He hadn't been able to do anything to fix it. So, he'd kept running.

Since then, the universe had only reinforced how helpless Joaquin was at being a protector.

The instinct to rush in the opposite direction was strong now too. There had to be someone else better equipped to deal with whatever was going on with their normally stoic grandfather.

Lifting his phone, Joaquin scrolled through his call list. His sister was his go-to when someone they loved needed emotional support, but today she was off limits.

He was on duty. There could be no evading it.

"Boy," the gravelly voice hollered at him from inside the dark room. "Stop sulking at the door and join me." His grandfather waved at the chair across from him.

Joaquin took a deep reinforcing breath and stepped into the room. "Tito, you're stressing the bride out. Abigail was expecting you—"

"I know." The old man waved off his words. "I just couldn't..." He shook his head, his lips pressed together. "Sit."

Work-worn hands shook as Tito lifted the lid of an old cigar box. "You're too tall. Y'all get that from your mom's side of the family. Did you know her father played in the NBA? Of course, that was before they made outrageous amounts of money for throwing a ball around. She didn't know him and her mother didn't have anything nice to say about the man who was her father."

Joaquin froze. "Why didn't she say anything?" As a teenager, Joaquin had dreamed of playing in the NBA. It had been his whole life until the accident.

Tito shrugged. "She didn't keep in contact with her family. There were issues. We became her family. She was the daughter Junie always prayed for. She didn't want to pass her bias on to you. Ironic that you never played another game after..."

Joaquin went to sit in the chair opposite, then paused. Distance was easier, but his gut told him his grandfather needed him closer. With trepidation he went against his normal response and sat in the chair next to his grandfather.

With a deep breath Joaquin scooted closer and put an arm around him. When a weathered hand patted him on the arm awkwardly, he knew he had made the right move. They were both out of their comfort zone. "So, tell me. What's in the box?"

"I'm not the one who should be here." Grief and guilt thickened Tito's every word.

"You taught me that God's always in control. If you truly believe that, then you're where you should be." That was also the reason Joaquin was scared to turn everything over to God. What if God's plan wasn't the one he wanted to live with?

He gritted his teeth and deflected that train of thought. Today was about his sister and grandfather. "Does the box have to do with Mom?"

"And your grandmother and my mother. Maybe before. I don't know. I never took the time to ask. Now there's no one who knows." He dropped his head. "The day we married, my mother gave this to my bride to wear. Then on the day your parents married, Junie gave it to your mother. I was there. She was so beautiful on all levels. We welcomed her as a daughter. Abigail looks so much like her."

Joaquin's mind filled with images he had locked away. His mother's love of music. She had believed there was always time for singing and dancing. The day they'd brought the twins home everyone had been so full of joy. Abigail's love of life and people, her social, outgoing personality, was so much like their mother's.

He swallowed the lump in his throat. His grandfather had a lifetime of memories. Did it make days like today harder?

"Diego had caused more problems. His drinking and gambling was getting worse. I tried everything I could think of to bring him back to the straight and narrow path. But then he took all that money the Zayases had given him for the land I had signed over to him and blew it on some big scheme to make more money. Gambling was also his solution, instead of hard work. He threw a fit of course and got in trouble. Your mother and Junie wanted to go get him, bring him home." Tito shook his head. Tears fell. "I was so angry at the shame he brought to our family. Drinking, gambling, then secretly getting married. He wasn't raised to act that way."

Joaquin pulled his grandfather closer. He'd never spoken of that time or really of any part of the past. The siblings had all followed the unspoken rule: the past was the past. No changing it, so don't waste time dwelling.

Joaquin's chest hurt from the pressure of emotion he'd spent the last twenty-eight years bottling up. "Tito, it's not your fault. He was an adult who made his own choices."

"Yes. But my pride had me sitting at home. Junie and your mom wanted to go get him. I said to let him rot. I refused to go. So, they convinced your father to drive them across the country to bring him home." His shoulders shuddered and for a second he leaned into Joaquin.

"My stubborn pride. Junie always said it would be the death of me. But it wasn't. My pride killed them. It should have been me."

"Tito. No." Grief and guilt swamped him, heavier than the day he'd found out about the accident. His lungs burned and he couldn't form the words he needed to soothe his grandfather.

"I was so useless and couldn't raise the kids. Cyrus lost his future in baseball to become a father to his siblings. I wasn't strong enough."

Joaquin's instinct to avoid his own pain warred with his need to relieve his grandfather of his guilt. He couldn't let his grandfather carry the responsibility alone.

"I left for the military five months after the accident. Everyone said I was brave serving my country, but it was a coward's move. I abandoned you and left Cyrus to pick up the pieces. I didn't want to deal with all the mess and chaos we had fallen into. It was my fault the accident happened and I couldn't deal with it so I abandoned you." He had never spoken of his guilt.

"No. Mijo, you were a boy becoming a man. I leaned on you too much instead of guiding you. If I had gone, then your father, mother and grandmother would have been here to do that for you and your siblings."

"Nope." Joaquin shook his head. "Losing you was not a better option. I always went with Dad on his long road trips when Cyrus left for college. We took turns driving, kept each other awake. But I didn't want to miss the stupid basketball tournament. I don't even remember if we won." His stomach twisted so hard he thought he might vomit. "We lost everything because of my selfishness." He had never voiced his darkest shame. "I'm so sorry, Tito."

"Oh no, mijo." Rough hands cupped his face and forced him to make eye contact. "We would have never expected you to tell your coach you couldn't go. That was a commitment you had made to your team."

"No matter what I do I can't keep anyone safe. How do you live with the loss?" He admired his grandfather so much.

Tito wrapped him in a bear hug and held him close. "Mijo, it's all about love. It took me too long to get over myself and focus on you kids. It was too late for you and Cyrus. The damage was done and I'm so sorry. Your grandmother would have kicked me. A large chunk of my heart went with them. But it wasn't forever. What I finally remembered was all the love and joy they brought into my life. I wouldn't trade anything for those memories. They're worth it all."

After the longest hug Joaquin had ever been a part of, he patted his grandfather on the back and they separated. He doubted the happy moments were worth the heartache but couldn't admit that to his grandfather. Locking his misgiving down, he deflected for now.

"So, why didn't you give this box to Cyrus's bride or Abigail at her first wedding?"

"Truly, I forgot all about it." He opened the box to reveal vintage diamond earrings and a ring. He shook his head. "Who would have ever thought it would be a Zayas that restored the family tradition?" He snorted. "Don't tell him, but I really like that kid. Your grandmother would approve. Being there the day your child gives their heart and future to another is truly a special time. It's different this time, maybe because the wedding is here on the ranch, or because of the family connection with the Zayases and the past. I woke up this morning remembering the earrings. I knew where they were too. It's like our family are here with us today, giving us their blessings."

Tito wiped his eyes with the back of his weathered hands. "Mijo, don't give up on finding joy in life. Yes, there's risk, but the memories make life worth living. My regret comes from my pride and not giving the people I love another chance. Don't hold yourself back from the fear of losing everything. Grief means we had the honor to love someone. Here. Take this." He pressed the ring into Joaquin's hand. "You'll probably be the next to get married. Promise me you'll open your heart to the possibilities right in front of you."

"Tito. No." Stopping himself from throwing the ring back, he slid it across the table to his grandfather.

His heart slammed against his chest thinking of slipping the ring onto Lali's finger. Her laughter surged to the front of his mind. Were she and Oscar worth the risk or would he lose them before they could even be his, like Celeste and Ethan?

"You have so much love to give mijo. Don't let my failures stop you from see the gift right in front of you."

With more strength than a old man should have, Tito firmly put the ring back in Joaquin's hand. "Share that love."

Not wanting this conversation to go on any longer, Joaquin slipped the ring into his pocket and stood. Today was about his sister.

"Come on, viejo vaquero. Let's go find the bride and soothe her unraveled nerves."

His own nerves could use some soothing. It was no use opening himself up to loving Lali and Oscar when they were going to leave soon, as was he. Did his grandfather know something he didn't?

Chapter Twelve

As the sun set behind the hills, hundreds of fairy lights lit up the ceremony. Abigail and Kingston stood under the ancient oak next to the fence that divided their properties.

They were surrounded by family and friends but only had eyes for each other.

Joaquin patted his grandfather's knee. The diamond earrings completed Abigail's ensemble beautifully. Joaquin glanced behind him to try to find Lali, but he didn't see her. Maybe she had finally had enough and was safely tucked away in the cabin.

The happy couple were introduced, then everyone followed them down the path to the Tres Amigos venue. There were about a hundred people. Abigail had considered it a small, intimate wedding.

For him there were about ninety people too many. But it wasn't his wedding. Not that he would ever have one. The one time he'd thought there would be a wedding, he'd pictured it on the ranch in the backyard with just his family.

Would Lali ever consider marrying again? He touched the ring in his pocket. Her track record was worse than his. He sighed. Why did he torture himself? Shadow nudged him and he patted the dog, reassuring him he was good.

"Joaquin," Oscar called.

He turned to the right. The boy was rushing to him holding Luna's harness. Lali was right behind him looking a little frazzled.

He stopped and allowed other wedding guests to pass him.

The old, restored barn was just yards away.

"I saw Leo." The boy hugged him. "He was in wedding clothes. So are you. I hated it when I had to wear them. Will you get to take them off soon?"

He gave Lali a worried glance. Her son wouldn't pick up on clues that the topic might be difficult for her. "I don't know. I think I look kind of sharp." He tilted his black Stetson to Lali and winked. "But I would rather be out riding with the herd."

"Momma says we can leave after dinner. Do you think Leo can leave with me?"

"We'll have to ask his mom." He looked at Lali. "How are you doing? You don't have to stay."

Her smile was weak. "No, no. It's good. I'm

great. It's a beautiful day and Abigail is stunning. I agree that the cowboy tuxedo is a good look."

"Momma, if you get married again, can I wear a cowboy tuxedo instead of a regular one?"

She laughed, but it was hard and stiff.

Leo poked his head out the side of the barn. "Oscar." He waved him over. "We have our own table. Come sit with me. Mom and Kingston are taking pictures."

He looked up at his mother. "Can I go, Mom?"

"Yes, yes." She waved him on.

Cyrus joined them and sighed. "Time to make small talk."

Joaquin groaned. "There has to be something else that needs to be done. Anything to avoid chitchat about the weather and how the football team will be better next year."

"I'm with you. I tend to bore people with my talk of mud and rock formations," Lali said.

Cyrus laughed. "Y'all have too much in common. My little brother here has been known to put people to sleep with how restoring native plants is good for the dirt." He winked.

"But it's true," Lali defended him.

"Then I'll leave you to it." He clapped Joaquin on the back and winked at Lali before he left.

"Sorry about my family."

Her features softened. "I like them. They're the kind of family I use to fantasize about having."

"You don't anymore?"

"Reality has taught me that we can't always have what we want. I come from a very academic family with a strong career orientation. That's what I know, so I'm not sure how I would manage outside of that world."

"Definitely different worlds. I barely graduated high school. Went right into the military."

"Hey, Joaquin. They're looking for you," Naomi interrupted. "Lali, you come with me. You're at our table and we want to ask questions about..." She glanced around as if she was in a spy movie. "Well, let's say if we found a cave here in the Hill Country. You can tell us what could be there, right?"

Lali laughed. He wanted her to laugh all day long.

"Yes. I can do that." She gave Joaquin a look of regret then went in with Naomi.

Was he reading that right? Fear tore at his gut. His grandfather had told him not to live in fear, but what if he opened himself to Lali and Oscar and then they left?

Could he put himself out there again?

He went inside and was swallowed up in all the wedding rituals until he finally was allowed to slink into the shadows. Cyrus followed him. "I'd give my kingdom for a cold drink and a quiet place to sit."

"In this we are just alike, brother."

Cyrus nudged him, then pointed to their sister dancing with her new husband. "If I didn't know any better, I'd say Tito masterminded this whole thing just so the ranch would end up back in our family bloodlines. I mean you do realize Kingston and Abigail's children will eventually inherit the ranch. He's playing the long game. One marriage at a time."

Joaquin laughed out loud, causing several people to glance their way, including his sister. He gave her a smirk and then glanced back to see where Lali was.

She was holding Oscar's hand and they seemed to be having a serious conversation. Did his grandfather really believe she was the one for him? She'd had a groom abandon her not that long ago. What was her first wedding like?

He glanced at his brother. "Can I ask you about Charlene?"

"Sure." His brother's eyes became guarded. "What is it?"

"Y'all were in college making plans for a very different future. Did you have any doubts about asking Charlene to marry you?"

Cyrus watched Emma for a little bit, who was arm in arm with Kingston's mother. "When I realized we hadn't just lost our parents but that I was going to have to come back to raise Lucas,

Abigail and Isaac, I broke up with her. Three kids on a half-run-down ranch in a small town. That wasn't the future she had dreamed of. So, I said goodbye. Never in a million years did I think she'd give up everything to help raise the kids. I was afraid that she'd start to resent me. Resent all of us. But she never doubted that being here with me on the ranch was where she belonged. Her faith was so strong all the way to the end."

"Looking back and knowing now how you would lose her, with Emma just a little girl, would you do it differently?"

His brother frowned. "You mean like not marry her? No. If nothing else there's Emma. But more than that. She—" He shrugged and studied his iced tea as if it had the answers. "I don't know. She just knew me. I could be me, which as you well know isn't always easy. But she let me be all of that. We were safe with each other. Our family... We're close, but emotionally we were taught to hold it all in. I didn't have to with her."

He sighed and scanned the crowd again. "Being a DeLeon is not easy." The corner of his mouth quirked up. "I can imagine being married to one is even harder."

"Tita and Mom seemed to have done it well. Charlene too."

"Yep. So, does this line of questioning have anything to do with an expert on caves who is hanging out on our ranch? I mean digging up a tree and planting it in front of the lodge is a pretty big gesture for a guest you didn't even want here."

Joaquin just grunted. There was no way to articulate what he couldn't sort out himself.

Lali was drained. The smile she had plastered on her face was starting to crack. But Oscar was having too much fun with Leo, so she went on the hunt for a dark corner table to hide at while everyone celebrated the wedding.

Without thought she scanned the room, seeking out Joaquin. He was standing alone watching his family from a distance.

He turned and started toward the door, then made eye contact with her and stopped. Someone came up to him and started a conversation. For a moment he looked away to greet the older woman. She recognized a forced smile.

Joaquin lifted his face back to her and held her gaze. He said something to the woman, but his gaze never left Lali. The older woman laughed then walked away.

Like a big cat on the prowl, he made his way to her. That predator move should have been scary, not captivating.

He stopped at her table. Her heart rate amplified its rhythm.

"Hey." Then he shifted on his feet, like maybe he wanted to escape.

She raised her brows. She hadn't forced him to come over here. "Hey."

"I figured you'd be gone by now. I was about to sneak out. Do you need a ride?"

She pointed to the well-lit lawn through the open door behind her. "Oscar's playing cornhole with Leo. I'm waiting until he's ready to go."

"You're at my favorite table."

A light laugh escaped, but she bit it back before it made her sound like a teenage girl with a crush. He was just being nice, not flirting.

"So, you like the dark corner far away from the chatter too. Then by all means join me." Her smile slipped a bit, and she looked away. Why was she asking him to do something she knew he was avoiding? "I mean if you want to. You were on your way out. Please don't feel you have to keep me company."

With a sigh, he slid his big body into the chair next to her. "Are you all right? It must be hard being at a wedding so soon after you..."

He looked away, up at the beams above them then out the door.

"After running away from mine?" She let it sink in for a moment. "I hate weddings. But after everything Abigail and Kingston have done for

Oscar and me it would have been rude to shun the invitation."

She crossed her arms on the table and leaned forward. He did the same, his gaze searching her face. What was he looking for?

"*Hate* is a strong word. I just..." She shrugged. "They haven't been the highlight of my life."

"How was your first wedding?"

"Oh, it was more of a rushed ceremony at a courthouse. My parents were trying to stop it. But I was intent on proving them wrong. They said he would ruin my career and distract me from my purpose in life."

"Your purpose?"

"They were so focused on their chosen fields of study they hadn't planned on having children. But when they'd realized I was on the way, they'd decided it was God giving them a gift to pass on their legacy. I was to put our name in the history of research. I would discover something so great that the world would take notice. They vowed to expose me to all the wisdom and knowledge of the world from the moment I was delivered into their arms."

"Wow. No pressure." Sarcasm dripped from every word.

She chuckled. "I didn't really know it wasn't a normal childhood. Not until later. I finished my first undergraduate degree when I was eighteen. While studying for my master's I made extra money tutoring. That's where I met Avery. He was always smiling. Nothing was too serious to make fun of. I thought I was in love. He took me out of my bubble and showed me another side of life."

"Your parents were not happy."

"That would be the understatement. When I turned twenty Avery told me I was an adult and could do what I wanted with my life. I thought I needed him to be free of my parents. At twenty I rebelled against everything they'd taught me and married him. It was horrible. Avery was the life of the party, but he didn't have a clue how to be an adult. I was responsible for the apartment, paying the bills, everything. When I complained about him spending more than we had he said I was cramping his style. Then I discovered I was pregnant." She took a breath and glanced at Oscar. "He wanted to terminate."

Joaquin took her hand. "I'm sorry. He didn't deserve you or Oscar."

"I went to my parents. Of course they had to do the whole we-told-you-so thing. They would take us in, but I had to get back on track."

"After that you were willing to try marriage again?"

"Matias and I have known each other for several years. Our research has overlapped. My parents love him. They came up with the idea that we should get married. They thought Oscar's problems were due to the lack of a strong father figure. They also blamed Avery's lack of pedigree. They don't even acknowledge he's on the spectrum. I was tired of trying to keep up with my research and being a single parent. Matias is a good man, and we work well together. My parents were also backing him for department chair."

She sighed. "An hour before the wedding, he came to me and said he was having doubts. I took the opening and ran."

"And you got lost on the ranch showing up at my door in all your wedding glory."

She couldn't help but laugh. "Not sure there was any glory involved. But I was happy to escape. I still believe in marriage, but going forward it has to be on my terms. What about you? Any weddings in your past?" she said as a flirty joke.

He leaned back and the friendly, curious expression was gone.

She was horrible at flirting. "Sorry. That was supposed to be a joke." She pressed her lips together and glanced over her shoulder. Oscar and Leo were on the edge of the lawn, lying flat on their backs looking up at the sky. Luna was right next to her son, her muzzle resting on his stomach.

Joaquin cleared his throat. His profile was

clean-cut. He had trimmed his beard for the wedding. His hair was still a bit long but was pushed back. The black cowboy hat looked like it was just part of him. When had the strong country man become her thing?

She was about to change the subject when he spoke.

"While stationed in San Antonio I fell for a woman who had a son about Oscar's age. He was completely deaf."

"That's why you know ASL."

He nodded. "I made them my life. All my free time was spent with them. I was about to retire from the military and thought it would be great to come home with a family and start a new chapter. I asked her to marry me."

"She said no?" Lali couldn't imagine being this man's world and walking away from him.

"She said yes. I called Cyrus but told him to keep it a secret. I knew it would shock everyone. She was going to come with me to visit my family and we would tell them together."

He swallowed hard and then studied his boots for a moment. Dread twisted her stomach. "I don't think I like where this story is going."

His stare was intense as he made eye contact with her. The green of his eyes had vanished, leaving them silvery gray. "Sorry. Didn't mean to make it so dramatic. As far as I know they're good. Living in Dallas. Ethan's dad heard we were getting married. He swooped in, promising to be a better man and father. Her family thought she should stay close to them and give him another chance. I was told not to contact Ethan. I wasn't even allowed to say goodbye to him. I wonder what he thought happened. I hope she told him I wanted to see him again. Losing the relationship with Ethan hurt more than the breakup with his mom."

Breaking eye contact, they both looked to the boys on the lawn. "Kids can be innocent bystanders in the world of adults," he said.

"I can't imagine how much that must have tore at you." She knew him enough to know that he took his relationships and responsibilities seriously. "Not even a letter or phone call?"

"Nope. The father said it would confuse him."

"Well, that ridiculous. Someone you love disappearing is confusing."

"I agree. But I didn't have any say in the matter. I was just an ex-boyfriend."

He was using this story to warn her and give her the reason he kept his distance. She got it. He had lost so much in his life. "I understand protecting yourself. Oscar has made so many new connections here. You said we could make this place our Christmas tradition. I like that idea. You've become very important to Oscar." Not to mention herself, but it was clear he didn't want any kind of romantic relationship.

As they watched the boys, Luna rolled onto her back and Oscar rubbed her belly. He was pointing to stars in the sky and Leo hung on every word.

"I've been talking to Valerie about placing Luna with Oscar full-time. I don't want to say anything until the details are worked out. But would you be okay with that?"

Tears burned her eyes. "Didn't you train her for a veteran?"

"That's how the organization is funded. I was about to record her as a nonviable candidate. Now it seems as if she was born for the job." He turned to the boys and dog. "Sometimes the world tries to tells us where we should be but it doesn't fit. My grandfather says we have to trust God. I think Oscar and Luna needed each other and God is making it possible. We just have to be open to a change of plan."

He grinned at her. An army of ants marched in her lower belly. Those words explained so much in her life. Nothing ever fit. Had she been forcing her foot into a shoe that wasn't hers?

She looked at the dance floor. So many new friends that made the world seem right.

Outside, Oscar sat up. He leaned into Luna then stood. He waved to Leo and made his way to her. "Mom. Luna's tired."

"I'm ready to leave this Popsicle stand too," Joaquin said. "I'll drive you."

"Popsicle stand?" Her confused son looked around. "I don't see one. I like orange."

"It's just a saying. I'm tired too and want to go home. We can leave together," Joaquin explained.

Her heart melted like those imaginary Popsicles. She sighed. There was research to finish, papers to write and grants to win. She couldn't hide on the ranch much longer. There was no way to make it work.

Chapter Thirteen

Joaquin pulled up to the steps of Lali's cabin. When had he stopped referring to it as Cyrus's? In the back seat Oscar was sound asleep with one arm around Luna and his head resting on her.

Lali sighed. "He's gotten so big I'll have to wake him up. Somehow I missed the last time I carried him from the car to his bed. It just slips by without any fanfare."

"The firsts are always easy to mark. So many last times slip by, and you don't see them coming until it's too late. It's only looking back that you see it."

He had too many to list. With his parents, his grandmother and uncle. He'd had no warning that the last time he took Ethan to the park it would be the final time.

"Will you promise me that y'all won't leave without telling me?" He knew the words sounded pathetic, but the thought of not saying a proper goodbye to either of them made him want to cry. And he did not cry.

"Of course. I promise. Same with you. If we're still here when you leave for Mexico, you will let us know, right?" Were her eyes glistening with moisture?

She turned from him and opened her door, and the new side step rolled out from under the truck. She laughed. "I have to say that does makes it easier to get in and out of your truck."

He didn't bother to tell her it hadn't been a problem until she and Oscar moved onto the ranch. He had done it for her.

Moving to the back passenger door he opened it and stared at the boy who had worked his way into his heart. He hadn't known there was still room left.

Carefully he undid the seat belt and lifted Oscar into his arms. The boy's head nestled on his shoulder as he gave a contented sigh.

"Oh, you don't have to carry him." She pulled her jacket tighter around her.

"It's not a problem."

The Christmas lights lit up the tree in the front yard and trimmed the house. Pride that he had helped do this had him standing a little taller.

Oscar's head popped up. "Joaquin!"

He stopped, afraid he had done something wrong.

"It's okay." Lali was right next to them. "You fell asleep in his truck. He's just carrying you into the house."

"But he told me about lying under the tree at night to look up at the lights. Remember? He's here. Can we? Please. I want to lie under the tree with Joaquin."

"Oh, sweetheart." She gave him a guilty glance. "It's late and Joaquin wants to go home." The boy didn't say anything, just sagged against him. He could feel the disappointment.

"How could I say no?" Joaquin smiled at her.

Her full lips opened to say something, but she just blinked several times. "Um, okay. I'll get a blanket."

It didn't take long. Lali had a thick flannel blanket spread out under the tree and Oscar crawled under.

Dropping to his knees, Joaquin rolled onto his back and scooted next to Oscar. "I remember this being much easier," he laughed. "Now I understand why Tito and Dad said they would watch from the sofa."

"Are you okay?" Lali asked from above them.

He shimmied his shoulders and then reached around to dislodge a rock. "Yep. I'm good."

"It's beautiful." Oscar's voice was low in reverence to the sight above them.

The rich velvet sky could be seen through the branches. For a moment Joaquin heard Tita playing the piano. He could smell the cookies that were just taken out of the oven.

The soft blanket on the hard wooden floors. A fire popping in the fireplace as Tito read the Christmas story from the children's Bible.

For to us a child is born. He could hear his grandfather's voice. "Do you want to hear the story that's the reason we celebrate Christmas?"

"Yes! Mom, join us." Oscar wiggled closer to Joaquin then patted the spot on the other side of him. "Joaquin is going to tell us a Christmas story."

It didn't take her long to get in next to them. The lights reflected all the beauty of her face and heart. She gasped. "Wow. This is…splendid. It makes us feel so small but at the same time a part of something so big."

"The stars are a big part of the Christmas story. That's why we put stars on the tops of trees."

Oscar grabbed Joaquin's hand in his right and his mother's hand in his left.

Joaquin cleared his throat and started the story his grandfather had told them every Christmas for the first seventeen years of his life. Had Tito carried on the tradition for Abigail and Isaac? Or had it been lost when they lost the core of their family?

For the love of his family, it was time to remember. Time to pass the traditions and love on to the next generation. Tita and his mother would be sad if they knew he had dropped the ball.

**

Lali couldn't take her eyes off the night sky. If she did, they would fall on Joaquin, and he would probably see the confusion. Today he had opened his heart and told her such a deep personal story.

He'd smiled, a real smile that had taken her breath away. But he hadn't stopped there. Under the tree, he had laughed. It had been rusty, but it was a beautiful sound. Just like his voice as he recited the Christmas story his grandfather had told them as children.

He was so deeply ingrained with his family that he didn't see what a source of joy he was for them and them for him. His voice faded away and they lay there in silence, her son holding her hand. A tear slipped from the corner of her eye.

"That was beautiful. Thank you for sharing." The words were hard to get past the dryness of her throat.

"Seems I put your little man to sleep. Let me get him to bed for you."

They scrambled out from the tree. Joaquin gently pulled the blanket then lifted Oscar against his chest for the second time tonight.

She went ahead and opened the door. Some primitive part of her brain loved the image of this big mountain man gently carrying her sleeping son to bed. He was a protector and provider.

Was that what this was all about? Her longing

for a man to take care of them? But in her core, it felt like it was so much more. Matias would have been a solid husband, but he didn't stir these emotions in her—emotions that were so foreign to anything she had ever experienced before.

She followed Joaquin into her son's bedroom and pulled back the weighted blanket. With a softness opposite his fierce size, he laid the much smaller body in the bed.

"Thank you so much for everything tonight," she said.

"Thank you." Then he left, softly closing the bedroom door behind him.

Lali busied herself by taking off Oscar's small shoes.

"Mom?"

"Hey, prince of my heart. Here's your pj's. Need help putting them on?"

"No, I got 'em." His sweet voice was slurred with sleep. "Is Joaquin still here?"

"He said good night then left. He thought you were asleep and didn't want to wake you."

"But Luna is here."

The dog looked up at her. Such intelligent eyes full of love for Oscar. "You're right. Maybe he's letting her sleep over."

"Can she sleep in my bed?" His head nestled into the pillow.

"Yes."

"Good. I love her and Joaquin." And with that final word he went back to sleep. The dog looked at her for permission and as soon as she gave it, Luna jumped up. After a couple of sniffs and a few circles she curled up next to him.

"I'm afraid I might love him too," Lali said quietly.

Leaving her son's room, she paused. Joaquin was in her kitchen. He had the kettle on and a couple of large mugs out.

"Hey. Did he stay asleep?"

"Um, he woke up enough to notice Luna, then went right back to sleep." No point in telling him what Oscar said. She would probably mess it up and let her feelings slip. "Luna is in bed with him. Do you want me to get her?"

"No. She can stay. It's getting hard to keep her separated from him. Before the sun comes up in the morning she's whining, wanting to see him. She pouts all night." He smiled and handed her a steaming cup of hot chocolate with a candy cane on the side.

"My mom loved stirring her hot chocolate with a bit of peppermint."

There was the elusive smile again. "Wow. Two smiles in one night. The wedding must have you feeling good."

"I don't think it's the wedding." He looked out of front-windows. "For the first time in a long while I'm enjoying Christmas. Want to go on the porch and finish off our drinks?"

With a nod, she followed him outside. "You must be tired. The brothers of the bride were very busy today. On top of your normal ranch duties."

He chuckled as he leaned against the railing and looked up into the sky. Without the obstruction of Christmas lights and branches it was vast.

"The number of stars is breathtaking." She kept her voice low.

He took a sip of his drink. "Before I left, I wanted to make sure you were good. It had to be hard being so involved in another wedding."

She looked to the hills. "It's been easy to focus on the cave and not think about it."

"Do you have any regrets?" He moved closer.

"Regrets?" She took a minute to really process, something she hadn't really given herself a chance to do. "That man didn't want to marry me. I realize that now. He was doing it to please my parents. I was doing it to make my life easier. That's not a reason to marry. I'm grateful he voiced his doubts before we made our vows. Can you imagine waking up the next morning knowing we made a mistake?"

"I can't image anyone being able to call you theirs and then saying it's a mistake."

Her heart slammed against her chest. She took a step closer. Her mouth was dry. She licked her lips. Never in her whole life had she initiated a kiss. But here on the hillside under the night sky and the magical Christmas lights highlighting his features, it seemed like the right thing to do.

She leaned closer then went up on her toes. Softly she pressed her lips to his and it was everything she had always imagined a kiss would be. The faint taste of chocolate and peppermint heightened her senses.

He lowered his head and took control. His hands held her steady. Time no longer controlled reality. A millisecond or hours. She couldn't tell.

When he stepped back the cold rush of air brought her back to the present. She touched her lips then looked up at him.

He had lost all coloring. He blinked a few times, maybe lost in the same time warp she had been trapped in. She couldn't read his expression, but it was obviously not happy.

"I'm sorry. It was just the..." She trailed off. What, the night sky made her kiss him?

"It's okay. Weddings have been known to do weird things to people and you were probably affected more than most. It's okay. Are you okay? I didn't..."

She snorted. "I don't really feel like myself right now. I'm not sure what's happening. I'm so sorry." She was sure he wanted to run.

Shadow came up next to Joaquin and nudged

him like he did when he was worried. She bit the inside of her cheek. The kiss had stressed him out.

How could she have made such a huge mistake? All these new and raw emotions had her acting out of character, but how did she explain that to him?

By the way, I think I might be falling in love. I've never really done that before. Yeah, I know. I've been married.

She was a mess. She needed time to analyze these new feelings.

He stared into his cup. "If you're good, I'll go home now."

The man was ready to run. She didn't blame him. With her best smile she nodded and took his empty mug. "I'm good. I'm tired. Very tired. So, I'll go in now. Thank you for everything."

He gave her that stiff half smile and jumped down the steps. He practically ran to his truck.

It would probably be best to avoid Joaquin for a while. Back to the reason she was here. There was an uncharted cave with history and secrets to unearth.

Facts were easier to deal with than messy emotions.

Chapter Fourteen

The sun was just peeking over the hills as Joaquin poured his second cup of coffee. He rubbed Shadow behind his ears. "What do I do now, boy? There're so many reasons we shouldn't even attempt a relationship."

But was that fear or facts? "Maybe instead of wallowing in my own thoughts I should talk to her." Last night he ran, as usual. "She's smart, compassionate and mature. Probably too smart for me. Why would she want to hang out with a guy who barely graduated from a small county high school?"

She was so different than any women he had ever met. "This self-talk is not getting us anywhere. Let's go. What's the worst that can happen? She tells me that she's not interested." He shrugged. "We can deal with that, right? It's all the what-ifs I don't want to live with."

Instead of taking his truck he walked to the lodge just up the hill from his. Three solid knocks and he put his head down, practicing what he was going to say.

The door opened and he looked up, making sure to smile. But it quickly turned into a groan.

"Well, this is an early-morning call, big brother. What, it's not me you wanted to see?" Lucas crossed his arms and leaned against the frame of the door laughing like a fool.

Great. His wise-cracking brother was the last person he wanted to deal with this morning. "Where's Lali?"

"She had some surprise visitors. I drove them up and now I'm watching the boys while she gives them a tour of the cave."

His brows furrowed. "No one knows about the cave. Are they from the university?" They had made a deal that no one else would be brought in unless they all agreed. It was already starting. People he didn't know were roaming around on his ranch.

"Oh, they're her parents and fiancé."

Joaquin's vision blackened at the edges and his internal organs froze. Shadow bumped his leg and licked his hand. He took three long breaths and blinked to clear his vision.

His younger brother narrowed his eyes and tilted his head. "Did you know there was a fiancé?"

"Matias. He's an environmental engineer also.

They share research. He's her ex-fiancé." Déjà vu threatened to swallow him into the abyss. His fingers balled into Shadow's thick fur.

"I don't think her parents know that. And she, um, didn't correct them." His brother stepped onto the porch and closed the door. Seriousness took all the humor out of his gaze. "I was getting a strong vibe between y'all. Was I imagining it? What's going on? I don't know what I would do if the girl I liked had a fiancé show up with her parents. That's tough. Are you okay?"

Joaquin lifted his hat and smoothed his hair back. His siblings knew he had struggled with PTSD. They didn't know the details and never pushed him, but they were there for him. They had always been there, even when he ran.

The sun washed the valley below in early-morning light. He didn't deserve their unwavering support. "I'm good. Just surprised by having visitors on the ranch and in the cave. Thanks for asking. Lucas?"

After a moment of silence his brother lifted his brows. "Yeah?"

"I just want to thank you for, um, always being there for me without question." His little brother had his own trauma. Only twelve years old, he'd been the lone survivor in the car accident that had turned their lives upside down. "I want to do the same for you. There's nothing you could say or do that would change how I feel about you. You know I love you, right?"

Lucas blinked a couple of times, and his throat worked up and down. Then he pulled out his famous grin. "Bro, it's too early in the morning for this—" he waved between them "—emotional bonding."

The door opened behind him. Leo, Oscar and Luna barged out. "Tio Joaquin! Oscar's abuelo and abuela are here. They're going to spend Christmas with us. And his mom's fiancé. But Oscar says he's not like Kingston." Leo giggled. "Except now Kingston is Mom's husband and my stepdad. When they get back from San Antonio, we'll be moving into the Tree House Cabin. It's at the highest point on the Tres Amigos Ranch. But I'll still be part of the DeLeon Ranch, right?"

Joaquin went down in front of the boys. Oscar was not making eye contact. One arm had a death grip on Luna, the other was pressed across his chest and he was tapping with both.

"Leo, you'll always be part of this ranch." Joaquin kept his voice low and even. "I know you're excited. But I think Oscar needs a quiet moment."

Bless Leo. He looked at his new friend and pressed his lips closed, then looked back at Joaquin with a nod.

They all stood still for a moment. Joaquin took deep breaths, encouraging Oscar to follow his lead. After a few beats, they were in sync. Isaac had taught him this strategy, so he used it to help Oscar regain self-control. Who was Joaquin kidding? He wasn't the only one who really needed to ground himself. Why did it feel like he and Oscar were a team and Matias was the enemy? He had to reframe the story.

"Oscar, are you okay?"

The boy still didn't make eye contact, but he nodded.

"Sorry. All the excitement wiggles inside me and I just let it go." Leo held his hand behind his back.

"It's okay, buddy. I came up to the lodge to see if there were any volunteers for ranch hands."

Leo shot his hand high into the air, but kept his lips pressed together. His sister was raising a good kid. "What about you, Oscar? I need to move the longhorns into a new pasture. You can ride Bucky again. He liked you. Or you can stay here with Lucas."

"Hey, why did you make that sound like a punishment?" His brother exaggerated a frown. "I would love to help you move your old longhorns. What do you say, Oscar? Sounds like fun?"

Joaquin tilted his head to Oscar. "You know Lucas doesn't do anything that's not fun. After the cattle are moved, we can check on the grasses and get some soil samples."

Oscar finally looked at him and grinned. "Yes."

Lucas laughed. "That boy is a clone of you. Who else in the world would be excited about soil samples? I think I'll leave that part up to y'all. I'll start prepping the waterlines for winter. There're rumors we might get one."

They headed to Lucas's truck. The thought that he and Oscar loved the same things twisted his already bruised heart. December 28 he would be heading to Mexico. It would be the best for all of them.

Lali switched the lights off as they moved past the area she'd started calling the grand hall. Her parents and Matias had been properly astonished by the findings of this cavern. It wasn't just an old cave.

But for her, the surprise and shock of them showing up unannounced was now melting into anger and indignation.

How could her parents just show up with Matias the day before Christmas Eve and act as if nothing had changed? They had even introduced Matias to Joaquin's family as her fiancé.

But in true Kan family fashion they'd focused on the opportunity for research and not the emotional upheaval a runaway bride might be going through. The lights on the helmets led them through the passages that hadn't been lit yet.

At least she wasn't confused about her feelings for her former fiancé. He was a good research partner but nothing more. She wanted the kind of marriage she saw with Abigail and Kingston. Someone to build a family and life with who had an impact even after they were gone, like Joaquin's grandparents and parents. The love that was built into the foundation and walls of Cyrus and Charlene's cabin, the only place she had ever felt at home in. She wanted a relationship that mirrored God's everlasting love.

They came into the next towering chamber, and she turned on the lights.

"This is amazing." Matias turned and looked from floor to ceiling. The surface glistened. It reminded her of the center of a geode when split open. "There are formations I've never seen before. The possibilities of new discoveries are..." He looked at her. "This is a large open space, but you don't come here alone, do you?"

"No. One of the brothers is always with me."

"They've given you exclusive rights to new discoveries?" her father asked as he moved closer to the wall. He didn't touch anything, but he was studying and taking pictures. "The potential of grants in cross disciplines is excellent. Any traces of Indigenous people?"

"No. We haven't discussed any legalities. The DeLeons just wanted an initial survey to get an idea of what we're dealing with. And they want it kept quiet." Her parents moved off to the far end of the long chamber. Then they circled around the formation in the center, a huge column almost six feet wide.

Her parents glanced at Matias and nodded as if encouraging him. Then they walked around to the other side, out of sight.

Matias took her hand in both of his. "Xitlali, we need to talk."

"Not really. You made a good call. There was absolutely no reason for us to get married and now we don't have to deal with divorce. We're good."

"I know I hurt you. If I had just calmed down and thought it through, I would have been fine. But I panicked. It wasn't a reason to end our relationship. We can still get married. All the reasons we were going to get married are still real and true." He took a deep breath and stepped closer to her. "Your parents understand your doubts after your first marriage, but I'm different. We balance each other."

She stepped back, pulling her hands out of his. "Everything you said that day was true. We're good research partners and friends. But that's not the kind of marriage I want. I wasn't hurt, Matias, I was relieved."

"Xitlali, you don't mean that. You're coming back to the university. That's where you belong. Not on some backwoods farm." His words sounded like a script her parents had prepared for him.

"Popi, Momi. Please stop pretending you're not listening."

Her parents joined them. "Mija. When you run off and make your own decisions, it doesn't go well."

She fought back an eye roll. That wouldn't prove her maturity. "Avery was a decade ago. I know I've made mistakes in the past, but I was young and sheltered."

Taking a deep breath, she smiled at them. This wasn't a fight. She would just state the facts. "I know what I want now. I love you, and the opportunities that you've given me have brought me to all the things that I'm passionate about. I want to stay here and do a deep dive survey of this cavern."

"Of course, mija. This is a great opportunity, but you don't have to stay in the cave. We'll get grants and you'll have students do the grunt work. You can collect the data, write the papers, speak at conferences. Share your findings with the world. It's been decades since a finding like this was available. You can lead that. You and Matias."

"I wanna be *in* the cave. I wanna stay here in Rio Bella. I wanna raise Oscar here."

With a gasp, her mother's hand went to her chest as if she had just heard death-blowing news. "You don't mean that. Oscar needs proper education and influence. He can't get that here in the middle of nowhere. I mean staying and observing for a little bit, yes. That's an irreplaceable experience that can enrich his education. But he can't be raised here."

Lali straightened her spine. "He's flourishing here. You're welcome to stay in my cabin for Christmas. And Matias can request a room at the DeLeons' main house. But I'm staying on at the ranch long term."

When had she decided that? She turned to leave the chamber. Had she fallen into the teenage-rebellion mode? Not a good place to make life-altering choices.

Her father frowned. "We've surprised you and you're just acting without thought. There's your grants and contract with the university. Let's take a break and then we'll talk about your future and how this cave plays into it."

She bit her bottom lip. They weren't going to make her do something she didn't want to do this time. Whatever she did was going to be on her terms.

"You're right I have to consider my current contracts. Either way, I'm glad you're here. It'll be nice to spend Christmas together if nothing else, right?"

They made their way back through the tunnels and she turned off the lights as they went. They used the rope that Joaquin had anchored here to help steady the uneven climb to the entrance.

Even though he had been against her coming he had made sure she was safe. She smiled at the memory of him grumbling over wearing the helmet when he took her down the first time.

They started making their way down the hill to the road and then she stopped. The sun blanketed a golden hue on the winter landscape.

In the pasture below, one tall figure and two small ones slowly moved away from them. On the edge of the road, three horses waited.

Observing every particle of his land, Joaquin strolled through the tall grass, his hands barely touching the top of the tips of the blades. On either side of him, the boys mimicked his movements. How did her mountain man make the job of checking fields so serene? The dogs zigzagged in front of them, noses on the ground.

He knelt and pointed something out to the boys. They were all huddled together. He put his hand out and Oscar opened the fanny pack he had slung over his shoulder. Together they used some sort of tool to put dirt in a bag.

"Who is that man with Oscar? And why is he running around in the field? Those dogs look dangerous. Do you know them? Are they safe?"

her mother asked, a touch of disdain in her voice. Lali had never been allowed to have any sort of pet. They were disruptive. Probably one of the reasons it had never occurred to her that Oscar could benefit from having a dog.

"They're trained service dogs. The man is Joaquin DeLeon, one of the landowners." And so much more. There was no way she was going to start a conversation about what Joaquin was to her or that Luna was about to permanently become part of the family.

Luna barked at them and all three turned and looked up. Joaquin stood. He handed the bag to Oscar, who put it in his pack and zipped it up. Leo waved and jumped up and down.

She waved and pointed to her Range Rover. Joaquin took the boys to the horses and helped them mount.

"Is Oscar riding a horse? Oh Lali, you can't let some strange man haul your son around on a wild ranch. It's too dangerous. Oscar is fragile. He can't handle an animal that size."

"Mom. Don't. Oscar is doing great. He's been taught horse safety and riding lessons from the best." Joaquin and Lucas had been diligent. "They would never put him in danger."

Her mother grumbled a few more sentences, but Lali only had eyes for the trio coming up to her car.

Joaquin was about to meet her parents and her ex. The swarm of butterflies had escaped her stomach and was fluttering up and down her spine.

Had it just been last night that they had kissed? But then she'd panicked and let him leave without giving him any indication of how she felt. Would he think she was a complete flake? It seemed a lifetime ago that she had stumbled onto his front porch in a wedding dress.

And now the man who she was supposed to have married was standing next to her. Joaquin had every right to doubt her intentions.

As the horses approached the vehicle, Joaquin tipped his hat to her parents and Matias. "Welcome to Rio Bella." Was she reading too much into it that he didn't include the ranch in his welcome?

She made the introductions. Then the awkward silence began.

"We've missed you, Oscar. Are you ready to go home?" Her mother moved closer to the horse, but then stopped. Oscar stared ahead as if he didn't see her or hear her. *Great.*

"Um, we're going to the cabin to get something to eat before we head to the main house. Matias will be staying there, in the extra bedroom upstairs." Why did she add that?

Joaquin looked down at her fellow scientist but

didn't say anything. Matias shifted closer to her. For protection? She kept her face neutral.

"Is that your home also?" her ex asked Joaquin a bit stiffly.

"Nope. I live there." Joaquin pointed to his small one-bedroom cabin. From here the hunting lodge was out of sight. Joaquin's gaze drifted back to her. "I'm going to join Lucas and Cyrus to help winterize the barns. They're predicting a hard winter storm to hit in the next couple of days. There's a good chance we'll be iced in."

"Oh no," her mother said. "That doesn't sound good. Maybe we should leave tomorrow."

Joaquin leaned forward and crossed his arms over the saddle horn. "That's probably good thinkin', ma'am."

She narrowed her gaze. Why was he exaggerating his accent? "I'll take Oscar with me now," Lali said. "I can take Leo too. Will you be able to get the horses back?"

"You can take Oscar, but Leo is part of the ranch crew, so he'll be staying with me."

"Oscar has to go with us," Leo argued. "He wants to learn how to winterize the barns."

Her son remained silent during the exchange. "Sweetheart," she started but her mother interrupted.

"Oscar is coming with us. He doesn't need to know about barns in winter." Her mother was sounding like a snob.

"Mom."

"Yes, ma'am." Joaquin dismounted and went to Oscar.

Her mother approached the horse also. "Oscar, dear. You mother says you've made headway in your conversational skills."

Her son grunted and crossed his arms. Lali closed her eyes. *Please, don't let all the progress we've made slip away in front of my parents.*

"Hey, buddy. It's okay." Joaquin said something in sign language, but with his back to her she couldn't tell what it was. Her son visibly relaxed. "Go visit with your grandparents. We have plenty of time to teach you barn stuff. Swing your leg over and drop to the ground holding the saddle. Don't let go of the reins but leave them loose."

He gently guided Oscar off the horse then took the reins. "Give Bucky a pat. He was a good boy for you today."

Oscar did as he was told then turned and hugged Joaquin before dashing to Lali's side. Luna stayed at his side.

"What's that dog doing?" her father asked, worry clear in his voice.

Oscar signed that she was his friend.

"Oscar. Use your words," her mother snapped.

"Luna and Oscar have become very close. Joaquin is training her as a service dog. She's incredible."

"She looks as if she could take his head off in one bite," Matias said, hanging back.

"Matias!" Lali wanted to get out of this situation.

"Yeah, she only bites on command," Joaquin added dryly.

Not helping, she wanted to tell him, but instead she smiled. "We're leaving now." She opened her back door and waved to Oscar to get in. She stopped Luna from following. "She's staying with Joaquin for now."

A flash of panic sparked in Oscar's eyes.

Joaquin was right behind her. "I'll bring her by after dinner. Is it okay if she sleeps over?" Both sets of eyes looked at her.

"Sounds like a good plan. Right now, we have to show off the ranch to our guests. We should go to Rio Bella for some lunch."

With that settled, Joaquin mounted and headed down the road with Leo and the now-riderless horse in tow. The dogs trotted alongside. Luna looked back a couple of times, but Joaquin called her attention back to him.

Lali's chest was so tight it was hard to breathe. Joaquin had to be wondering what was going on and with his history, he had to have doubts. Her parents had the worst timing.

Every cell in her body screamed to call him back, to take Oscar and get in that empty saddle and leave her parents and Matias to fend for themselves. It wasn't her fault they just showed up.

She had a life she was straightening out, and she wanted to do that with her grumpy mountain man.

"Lali, dear. Are you okay?" Her mother put a hand on her shoulder.

Nope. She was far from okay. But the person she wanted—needed—to talk to was riding away.

Chapter Fifteen

Joaquin lifted the bale of hay and tossed it into the back of his truck harder than required.

Last night when he had dropped Luna off with Oscar, he had interrupted a cozy family chat about research grants. He had gotten out of there as quickly as possible. Lali had started to follow him to the door but her father had asked her to pull up a file or something on her laptop. He had not stuck around.

The forecast said a heavy winter storm was on the way, so there was plenty to do to keep him busy and his mind off Dr. Xitlali Kan. He might even have to miss the family Christmas Eve dinner.

He chucked another bale of hay as hard as he could into his truck.

"Christmas Eve gift," Abigail yelled from the front of his truck.

He turned with a scowl. "What are you doing here? Kingston was supposed to keep you in San Antonio until sundown."

"Love you too." She walked to the stack of hay and slipped her gloves on, then hefted a bale into the bed. She climbed up into the back of his truck and started to arrange the haphazard mess he was making.

"Leave it. It's fine."

With her lips pressed downward, she gave him a side-eye. "Oh, thank you for asking. We had an exceptional evening then a beautiful breakfast on the riverwalk. That's where we heard the weather report. Kingston didn't want to leave Naomi and Letti alone to deal with it, not after the flooding. And I thought y'all might need some help too. How is everything? You seem more out of sorts than usual."

"I'm fine."

"The hay is fine. You're fine. So, this doesn't have anything to do with our surprise Christmas guests?"

"It's Christmas Eve. Shouldn't you be bothering your son or new husband? This isn't your home anymore."

"Wow. You must like her more than I thought. What? Do her parents not approve of you? What's going on? You had become, well, happy. Why are you slipping back into Mr. Grumpy Pants?"

He tossed another bale, careful not to hit her. If he didn't say anything she'd get the hint and leave.

After stacking the hay, she turned to him, hands on her hips as she waited. Yeah, she wasn't going anywhere.

"So, her parents are here. And I was really surprised when I was introduced to her fiancé. Did no one tell her mother the wedding was called off?"

He almost grinned.

"He's not what I was expecting. Doesn't seem her type at all. What do you think?" His little sister was not going to let this go.

"None of my business. Did you come back just to harass me?" he grumbled.

She jumped off the tailgate and stood in front of him. "I say it *is* your business. Since she arrived, I've seen the shift in you. Not to mention the bond you've built with her son. How can you just ignore that?"

He wanted to hurl a bale of hay across the barn and scream. To rip something apart. "Doesn't matter. They'll still walk out of my life without a backward glance." He ran the back of his hand across his face.

Closing his eyes, he jammed the feelings back down. Letting emotions boil over like this wasn't good for anyone. He counted to twenty, then counted again. Shadow pressed against him and nosed the hand dropped at his side.

"I'm sorry," Abigail said. "I didn't mean to

push you. You were happy. You deserve to be happy."

She crushed her body against him and wrapped her arms around his neck. The embrace was so fierce it pushed to his core. "You're such a good man. Please don't let insecurity or pride or whatever it is you're battling win. It'll steal your happiness if you let it."

It wasn't true. He was nowhere close to being a good man, but he couldn't tell her that. His sister was on a wedding high. She found a good man. They were going to have a great life together.

He pushed aside the echoes of what his grandfather had told him about living in fear. This wasn't about that or insecurity. Maybe a little pride, but it was reality.

"You sound like Tito. Not all of us are meant to be paired off. It's okay. I have a complete life I've carved out for myself. The ranchers in Mexico need my help. That gives me purpose and makes me happy. My longhorns, my mustangs, my dogs, the healthy grasses and soil are all things that bring me joy. And I've got the best niece and nephew in the world."

She crossed her arms and steadied him for a while. His little sister was tough. She had to be after being raised by older brothers and a grumpy grandpa. But she still had the biggest heart.

He hugged her then stepped back. "I love you

too. Stop worrying about me. You've got enough on your hands being married to a Zayas and raising that high-energy boy of yours. Now are you gonna help me get this hay to the south barn or you just here to look pretty?"

"I'll go with you. I don't want to risk running into our guests again. They were hanging out in our kitchen."

"What were they doing in the kitchen?" That wasn't jealousy, it was just... Okay, so he hated the idea of Lali with Dr. Mini in his family kitchen. He smirked at his own joke. The man was a copy of her parents and he was small. Ha.

"Did you just randomly laugh?" Now she looked concerned. So did Shadow.

"In my head I keep coming up with nicknames for the groom Lali ran away from. I just called him Dr. Mini. Because he's small and a carbon copy of her parents. That's funny. It's a winner."

"No, it's childish. And he's not small. You're just freakishly big."

"Are you defending him?"

"They were drinking coffee and talking with words I couldn't decipher. I'm pretty sure it was English, but on a whole other level. They were working on her laptop."

Science stuff. That's what they were doing. He didn't want to think about what Lali and Matias had in common.

Abigail went on to talk about Christmas and Kingston and other things, but all his brain wanted to focus on was the fact that Lali and Dr. Mini were in his family kitchen talking science. She was probably remembering why he would make a perfect husband.

There was nothing perfect about an uneducated rancher with PSTD who disappeared when life got too murky.

Abigail started talking about the plans for tonight. "When we finish here can you take me to the Tres Amigos?"

"Sure."

When they returned to his truck from the barn she was quiet. "Abigail?" He should leave it alone, but he didn't want her unhappy.

"You've always had reasons to be gone on Christmas Eve, but you'll be with us tonight, right?"

No, no, no, no. Her eyes were wide and had tears threatening to fall. They were so much like their mother's eyes. "Yes. I'll be there before dark."

She recovered so fast he narrowed his eyes at her. "Did you just play me?"

"Of course not. You'll bring your guitar?"

He could do this. He'd focus on his family and making sure Oscar had the best Christmas Eve ever. He did grin at that. A couple of days ago, he had made it official with Valerie. Luna was going to be Oscar's dog. He had a big red bow for the occasion.

He couldn't wait to see the boy's face when he found out. Even if Joaquin didn't get to see him again, he would know that Oscar would think about him and how much he cared whenever he hugged Luna.

That would have to be enough.

Lali's father kept checking his phone. "The weather is turning bad faster than they originally predicted." He checked his phone again as they walked up the steps to the main DeLeon home.

"Gustavo, they love to hype these reports. This is Texas. We've been in Alaska during winter storms. Put your phone away. You're obsessing," her mother countered again.

If bickering was a love language it would be her parents'. Oscar tapped his fingers next to his collarbone.

"I should be booking a flight and driving to the airport instead of attending a party," he grumbled, fighting for the last word.

"We're not here for a party. Matias hasn't had a chance to convince our daughter—" She tilted her head and wiggled her fingers as if Lali wasn't standing right there.

"Mother. These people have become very important to me. I really—" The door opened before she could say anything else.

"Christmas Eve gift!" Abigail hugged her, then stole one of the gingerbread cowboys Lali had made earlier with Oscar. "Oh! They're little cowboys. I love it." She bit the head off. "These are so good," she mumbled. "Come in."

"I'm sorry we're early but—"

"No worries." Abigail cut her off. "We have an open-door policy. Oscar, Leo's in the back game room."

With one nod from Lali he was off. Abigail herded them into the kitchen. An all-you-can-eat buffet was covering the large island and parts of the table.

Lali couldn't stop herself from searching for Joaquin. Not here. Was he staying away because of her?

"Here are the plates. My brothers haven't swooped in yet, so get everything you want now. Don't be shy."

"This is a delight." Her mother's eyes were bright with curiosity. "Remember that time in Peru? They had a spread like this for their Christmas Eve celebration. Of course, I think we ate guinea pig."

Lucas came in through the back door. "Guinea pig? We might have some hog head, but no guinea pig." He screwed his lips to the side. "Where's Mateo?"

"Matias," her mother corrected. "Her fiancé.

He texted he'd be down soon. He hasn't done a great deal of field work, so he's not as used to these types of gatherings."

Lucas blinked. Then he looked at Lali. "She knows you ran away from that wedding?"

This was supposed to be a joyous celebration, but her head was already hurting. "Mother, Matias is not my fiancé. Please stop calling him that."

Her mother sighed and put a deviled egg on her plate. "I just think you were too quick to call it off. He's here and wanting to forgive you. He understands why you might fear getting married again."

Lucas leaned back on the counter and popped a sausage ball in his mouth. His gaze darted from her mother to her.

She sighed. "He's the one who called it off and I'm glad he did." She tried to keep her voice low and even. "We were never in a romantic relationship and…" Why was she even trying to explain? "I'm not talking about it. We're not getting married. Ever."

"Oh sweetheart, I know your first marriage was a nightmare. You were too young. But this is a solid relationship. A lifelong partnership that would benefit your career and Oscar. As parents we worry, and Matias would lift that burden from us. We want to know you're taken care of."

"Matias doesn't want to be Oscar's father. Anyway, Luna has helped Oscar more than anything else we've done."

"That big dog? That's ridiculous. Oscar needs routine and discipline," her mother said for the one-hundredth time. "Not a dog."

Joaquin came in from the back and stopped when he saw her. He was stiff and looked ready to bolt. His knuckles were white from gripping his guitar case. Shadow leaned against his leg. With his free hand, Joaquin made physical contact with his dog. Luna was on the other side of him, actively scanning the area. Looking for Oscar. Joaquin signed, *Go*. Nose down, she rushed into the living room and disappeared down the hall.

Lucas patted him on the shoulder. "Hey brother. Good to see you."

With a nod, Cyrus came through and filled a plate before heading into the living room. "Come on, Joaquin. Get some food, then play some music and set the mood."

Sofas had been pushed back to create more space around the large tree. Several chairs from the kitchen and other rooms had been added. Since they finally had some cold weather, a fire was blazing. Kingston and Abigail sat on the hearth eating, looking totally in love. Their grandfather had a plate balanced on his knee as he told Emma a story of her first Christmas.

Joaquin sat on a wooden chair slightly separated from everyone. He strummed a few notes on his guitar. Requests were made and voices joined his music as they sang several traditional Christmas songs. Oscar and Leo came in and sat on the floor right next to Joaquin's leg.

Oscar was much more relaxed than he had been all day. Truthfully, in a way he hadn't since her parents' arrival.

Across from her, Matias and her mother were in deep conversation. Then he got up and made his way around the back of the room to her and placed a hand on her shoulder. She frowned. What were they up to?

"Lali, I think your father's right. The forecast has moved up the timetable for the winter storm and it looks to be hitting hard by morning. We don't want to be stuck out here. They want to leave."

"Okay." She tried to keep her face neutral and not look too happy. It would be nice to have the DeLeon family all to herself again.

"Since we have to drive to San Antonio for our flight, I thought that would give us plenty of time to talk about our future."

The drink she was about to sip stopped halfway to her mouth. She couldn't have this conversation here, but it would have to be now. Standing, she went into the kitchen, and he followed. Her parents were right behind him.

Once on the far side of the kitchen, she turned around. "Oscar is excited about Christmas morning in the hunting lodge. We aren't going. There are a few more things I want to document in the cave. I'll be back at university before the new term starts."

"There is too much to do for one person. There needs to be a team and support. Come back with us and you can put that together." Her father gave her his no-nonsense stare that intimidated everyone, including her. "Xitlali, you have responsibilities and need to finish the other research commitments you've made."

She hated that he was right. Sound, logical reasoning on what she should do. But her heart didn't agree. How to explain without sounding like the immature girl she used to be?

She sighed and looked into the living room. Warm and cozy, the DeLeons were singing another song and the lights of the Christmas tree sparkled in her son's eyes.

Her mother stood closer to her. "You need to come back and set things straight. Even if you decide not to marry Matias. Your reputation as a top researcher is on the line. Playing in the cave is fun, but it's a waste of your time."

They were right. This could threaten her status in their academic circles. But she couldn't find it inside her to care. Her eyes widened. It hit her like a bolt of lightning.

She didn't care. The smile was hard to hold back, but she had been fretting and debating what she should do. It wasn't her desires battling each other. It was her core passion, the desire God had planted in her heart years ago, fighting against her parents' plans for her.

She nodded. They had one thing right. The sooner she went back the sooner she could put her old responsibilities behind her. She could have an in-depth face-to-face conversation with Dr. Flores. He was chair of the environmental engineering department. With his connections she would be able to design a plan of action that was best for the cave and the families involved.

It would also give her time to figure out her feelings for Joaquin. Well, she knew how she felt. The problem was what to do about it. He had turned a cold shoulder to her.

Matias put a hand on her arm. "I think it's best if you come with us tonight. If you stay, there's no telling how long you'll be trapped here." His expression was clear. He thought being stuck here on the ranch was a nightmare. But to her, it was her dream.

But it couldn't happen yet. "I agree that I need to go back."

In unison her parents let out a sigh of relief.

"I knew you wouldn't disappoint us again. This is the right thing to do." Her father looked so proud of her.

Her mother was about to speak, but Lali cut her off. "But not for the reasons you've argued." She glanced at Matias then her mother. "One, we're never ever going to be anything more than co-researchers, so don't mention that again. Two, I'm not staying at the university. I'm changing my field of study. I'm going to consult with Dr. Flores. But no matter what, Oscar and I will be moving to Rio Bella. Even if that means I teach high school science."

Horror etched its way to every line on her parents' faces. She held firm. "No arguments."

"Xitlali, you have a responsibility to your heritage and your family name." Her father's stern face would have had her cowering in the past.

"Sorry, Popi. I'm taking responsibility for my future and my son's. I'm listening to God now and following the path He's laid out in my heart. Tonight, we'll go with you so I can take care of past business. But I have a new path."

Her mother placed a hand on her father's arm, and without a single word told him to back down for now. He gave a subtle nod. Lali knew it was temporary. But at this moment she had won. She was going to take it and run.

"Thirty more minutes here, then we'll go to

the cabin to get our bags." Her first instinct was to tell Joaquin that she knew where she was supposed to be.

She hoped he'd be proud of her. But then again, Abigail had told her Joaquin was leaving for Mexico sooner than expected. Would it change his mind if he knew she was staying? She sighed.

He had his own complicated emotions to work out. Maybe they both needed this time away.

If she left with her parents tonight, she would be the one leaving first. She scanned the room for Oscar, intentionally not seeking out Joaquin.

Oscar would be upset with the new plan. Would Joaquin care? He'd probably be happy. He'd never wanted her here before things got complicated.

He was leaving too. He didn't need a special announcement.

The pit of her stomach twisted. They needed time. She would be back and so would he. That would be a new start. But first she had to clear the old path to make way for a change in course.

Chapter Sixteen

Joaquin needed fresh air. Air that wasn't full of Christmas joy and family laughter. Had Lali's parents and Matias convinced her to leave tonight with Oscar? The four of them all huddled together in the kitchen couldn't be good. They were from her world and wanted to take her back to her natural habitat.

The ranch, his family and Joaquin were just a temporary layover.

A heavy fist pushed on his ribs, making it hard to breathe. Shadow was butting his head against Joaquin's leg.

Shadow licked his hand as he slipped out the screen door. "Thank you, boy."

He stopped when he saw Oscar by the back gate. Luna was blocking him from opening it.

"Oscar?" Why was the kid out here alone?

Luna barked. She ran halfway to him, made a low, rumbly bark in the back of her throat, then ran back to Oscar.

"What are you doing?"

"Going to the cave." He sounded upset.

"You can't go into the cave without an adult or at night." Was he really trying to use logic instead of just telling him to come back inside?

"It's not dark yet. Momma has helmets with lights so when the sun goes down we can see. You're an adult. Let's go." He pushed at the gate.

This was one of the most bizarre conversations he had ever had.

"I'm texting your mom and letting her know where you are."

"No." Oscar was uncharacteristically angry.

After hitting Send, he slipped the phone into his back pocket. "Why are you hiking to the cave on Christmas Eve?"

There was a long moment of silence. He was about to restate the question, when Oscar grunted and shook his head. "I don't want to leave the ranch. Matias wants us all to go right now. I heard Momma say okay. But she loves the cave. I'm going there until she agrees to stay with me."

She was leaving tonight? Shadow barked at him.

Pushing past the punch to his gut, he placed a hand on Oscar's shoulder. "Running away from your mom isn't the best solution. You need to talk to her."

"My friends are here, you're here and Momma's happy. We stay."

Joaquin wanted to hug him tightly and promise that he would always be here for him. But that was a vow he couldn't make. He wasn't his father and had no right to make any kind of promise.

"Not talking about your feelings to your mom isn't good for either of you." *Yes, God, I know I'm being a total hypocrite.* "I know, because I tend to run from things I don't want to deal with."

Oscar crossed his arms and looked at him.

"It's not a peaceful way to live your life, trust me. I've learned that the hard way." He was starting to believe it, and now he needed to live it.

After a long moment, Oscar said, "I trust you."

The simple words literally brought Joaquin to his knees in front of the boy who had claimed real estate in his heart. They were more powerful than *I love you.* Not able to stop himself, he pulled the boy to him and hugged him.

"No matter how far away you go, you can call me, and I'll be wherever you need me. Always."

He leaned back and studied the boy. "You might have to physically leave with your mom, but I'm just a phone call away." He knew without a doubt that Lali would not cut them from each other's lives. Wherever she might have to go she would value the bond he and Oscar had, even if she didn't love him back.

Love him. That twisted his already-tender gut.

He loved her. It didn't matter how much he had tried to stop it; it had happened.

God, may Your will be done. If I'm not to love her remove this feeling from me. Let me handle it with serenity and wisdom.

Joaquin stood and held out his hand. "It's too cold to be standing out here. Let's go to the porch." Oscar took his hand and followed along the stone path leading back to the house.

"Sometimes the people we love might not be in our lives every day. At your age, you have to stay with your mom. But you also need to talk to her. It's okay to be sad or upset."

Oscar had his arms crossed and was tapping his fingers. "What if I never come back? What if she marries Matias? Luna lives on the ranch. I want to walk the fields with you and check on the herds and ride horses."

He wanted to comfort them both and assure Oscar his mother wouldn't go back to Matias. They shared a common language and education. Would she fall back into her parents' plans and marry him? "Your mom did say y'all might come back next Christmas. You need to talk to her about that. She's passionate about the cave. If y'all leave tonight, she'll be coming back for no other reason than to finish her work." Was he giving himself a pep talk?

Oscar pointed to the sky. "The moon and stars

are playing hide-and-seek behind the clouds. Look! It's Sirius. Can you see it?"

"Which one?"

"The brightest one. Draw a line through Orion's Belt." Oscar moved his finger across the sky.

"The Christmas story has a bright star that led people to baby Jesus." Joaquin studied the stars with a new appreciation. "Over two thousand years ago they looked at the sky the way we're doing right now. God's creations are amazing."

"And everlasting," Oscar added.

"You're right. Through Him we are also. We're connected. No matter how far away you are, look up and know we are looking at the same sky."

Joaquin didn't want to think this could be their last time together. He had to trust God that if Oscar was meant to stay in his life he'd be back. He thought of Ethan and prayed the boy was well and happy. Just because they had only been temporarily in each other's lives didn't mean it didn't matter, or that they weren't impacted.

It was time to let Oscar go. "It's getting colder. Ready to head back to the house?"

"No. But it's the right thing to do."

Joaquin laughed. "Truer words have not been spoken."

The screen door slammed open. "Oscar. Why are you outside in the cold?" Lali went to the bottom step and flung her arms wide. Oscar ran to her and she pulled him close. "I couldn't find you and I was so worried."

Joaquin wanted to join them, wrap them in his arms and never let go. But he had to, like he'd had to let go of his grandmother and his parents. And Celeste and Ethan.

It hurt to let go of people you loved, no matter the situation or reason. He never seemed to have a choice. A month or two in Mexico and he'd recalibrate and maybe he'd have this feeling under control.

But he wasn't strong enough to watch them leave without saying something he shouldn't and embarrassing them all.

A nighttime ride sounded like the perfect way to distract himself while Lali and Oscar drove away.

Lali held her son close, then looked up to tell Joaquin what she had decided, but he had turned his back and was already at the gate. He didn't pause or look back. He disappeared into the dark cold night. Without a word or even one backward glance. He was done with them.

The depth of the pain was unexpected. Would her being here stop him from enjoying the holidays with his family?

Holding her son close, she led the way back into the house. "Oscar, we're leaving tonight."

238   *The Rancher's Christmas Gift*

His eyes went wide. Crossing his over his torso, he tapped his fingers rapidly on his upper arms. "Luna?"

She closed her eyes. This had been her fear. Once again she'd put them in a bad situation and Oscar was paying the price. She could deal with a wounded heart, but her son?

Her father walked in. "Flights have been cancelled. But I booked us a room in San Antonio. Everything should be on track in the morning." He noticed Oscar's meltdown. "What's wrong with him?"

She was too fragile to handle her parents or Matias tonight. "He's overwhelmed with the changes. I'm not sure what we are going to do." She looked at her watch. "I'm taking him to our cabin."

Her mother reached for her arm and pulled her close. "Mija, you need to be strong when he behaves like this."

She hugged Oscar close to her and pressed her hand on his back to comfort him. "Mother." She kept her voice low and soft. "I know what my son needs. When I decide what we are doing I will text you. Don't wait for us. We'll meet you at the airport."

"Mija, you're so stubborn." Her mother crossed her arms. "We should travel together. There are things to discuss."

Her mother wanted to keep her close in hopes she could wear her down. "I'm not arguing about this. I called Dr. Flores earlier. We're going to meet in a couple of days. I have a plan."

Oscar still had his arms crossed over his chest, but he wasn't tapping. "Luna?"

She knelt to make eye contact with her son. With Luna sitting next to him, it was harder to look into the dog's eyes than her own son's. "She belongs on the ranch with Joaquin."

Both looked as if they were going to cry.

Her parents left. Her mother was sure to update Matias, maybe even develop a plan to get her in the car with them. She needed to leave now before that made this more difficult.

Oscar signed Joaquin's name.

She couldn't allow herself to cry. Not here. "He left. He'll be in Matamoros, Mexico, soon. He has a job there. How about you call him tomorrow when we get settled? Hug Luna goodbye."

The sight of her son and Luna broke what was left of her heart. She didn't have the energy to say goodbye to everyone, so she pulled Abigail aside and thanked her for everything.

"What about Joaquin? Have you told him?"

"I don't think he wants to speak to me right now."

"He can be stubborn and talking to people is a rusty skill. Don't give up on him."

"He has my number, so he can call if he wants to talk."

One last hug, then she had Oscar strapped into the back seat. She slipped into the driver's seat and headed down the long, winding dirt drive. Sleet started pinging the windshield. "No. This was supposed to hit tomorrow."

Her stomach was in knots as she left the ranch and turned onto the county road.

Was she being a coward? Overanalyzing was not going to help. Joaquin was going to Mexico. He had rearranged his life to avoid her.

"Mom, look!"

Was Joaquin coming after them? She glanced at the rearview mirror and narrowed her gaze. There was no way she saw what she thought she was seeing. Luna. Running full out on the road.

"She doesn't want me to leave her. You have to stop. She could get hurt or lost."

Lali pulled onto the narrow shoulder. Oscar was twisted as far as he could in his seat looking out the back. The poor dog was in danger trying to catch up to them. Ice was already forming on her coat.

She didn't have the courage to go back to the ranch. But that dog was going to follow them until she dropped dead from exhaustion or exposure.

As Lali stepped out of the car, Luna charged at

her. "This is extreme even for you. You're gonna get us all in trouble."

As soon as she opened the back door, Luna jumped in, licking Oscar's face. "I missed you too." Oscar hugged the dog like he was never going to let her go.

She sighed as she got back into her car. She rubbed her hands to warm them up. They would have to leave Luna in Rio Bella tonight. Maybe at the feedstore. Thalia had seemed helpful on her delivery trips to the ranch.

The sleet came down harder. She'd been in worse weather. She'd get them to San Antonio safely. She just had to stay focused.

Chapter Seventeen

With each sway of the horse's movement, the leather flexed and creaked. Shadow trotted alongside the horse, panting.

At the edge of the cliff, Joaquin stopped and studied the river below. Dismounting, he dropped the reins and made his way down the to the cypress roots growing into the riverbed. This had been their favorite place to sneak off to growing up.

He huddled deeper into his coat. This was not the weather for hanging out on the riverbank, but he was so cold on the inside he almost didn't notice the sleet coming down.

This land belonged to the Zayas family now. The usual bitterness didn't flare up. He grinned. With his baby sister marrying the Zayas heir, it was back in the family.

Which was a good thing, because at this rate Emma and Leo would be the only ones left to inherit what was left of the ranch.

Lucas claimed that the world was too messed

up to have kids, Isaac had no interest in relationships and Joaquin...well, he obviously wasn't meant to settle down.

Noise from above broke into his downward-spiraling thoughts of a bleak future. "Joaquin? We come in peace." That was his brother Lucas.

"Don't be a fool," Cyrus grumbled.

"Hey. I don't want to be in a police report that states I was accidentally shot by my brother," Lucas replied.

"Who said it would be an accident?" Cyrus clipped back.

Joaquin glanced around trying to find an escape, but he was pinned down unless he dived into the river. The Frio was cold even on a hot July day. Tonight, he'd end up with hypothermia.

He sighed. "I'm unarmed, so the only accident you'd have is falling and hitting your fool head on a rock."

"There's the grumpy old man we all love. I told you he'd be here," Lucas carried on.

Cyrus sighed with the weight he'd carried on his shoulders for way too long. "Stop talking for five."

As they made their way down the slope, Joaquin blocked out their bickering and focused on the sound of the Frio running over the water-worn rocks.

Once they were down, Lucas slipped off his boots and stood on a large flat rock wedged between several roots. It made a perfect platform for jumping off or just dangling your feet in the river on a summer day.

"Now this would make a perfect ice plunge." Lucas proceeded to dunk his feet in the cold river. "Paw-aaa-wheee!"

"Cold, is it? Go ahead, jump in and swim down the river," Cyrus grumbled. "I should have come alone."

"You don't think I will?" Lucas grinned. "I've done colder plunges then this." He kicked his bare feet. "It clears the brain and jolts you into the present. Good for inflammation too. Lots of rodeo guys declare it keeps their bodies working. The three of us should do it. Great bonding."

"Staying off bulls would help the body and the brain," Cyrus shot back at him. The family had been after Lucas to stop bull riding since the day he started.

"We aren't here for my intervention. We came to save Joaquin."

He frowned. "I don't need saving."

Shadow gave a short bay, as if Joaquin was deep in denial. He glared at his dog.

"Shadow knows what's up. He's a smart dog trying to save your hide. You should listen to him." Lucas splashed water at him.

"Stop it." He wiped the water drops off his face.

Cyrus shook his head. "Lucas, you're not helping." His older brother sat on the root next to him and patted Shadow. "We're worried about you. You have a long habit of running when...when things get too heavy. Or you think you can't deal with what's about to happen. It's a survival mode that has worked for the most part."

He couldn't deny his brother's words. Joaquin put his hand on the back of Shadow's neck and buried his fingers in the thick black fur. He'd abandoned his family when they needed him the most. He'd left Cyrus to carry the majority of the burden alone. "I'm sorry. I should have been here for..."

"Don't. You did what you had to do. We all did. This is not about making you feel guilty for the past. You do that all on your own. This is about your future," Cyrus said as they both stared into the Frio, the river their family had settled on generations ago. Family members had come and gone but the river and the land were still here.

"Christmas is a time of honoring the gifts God has given us. A time to hold family close. God gave you a huge gift and you're letting her leave the ranch without telling her how you feel. Acknowledging the gift God brought to your doorstep should be the least you do. It's not fair to them either."

"He's talking about Lali and Oscar," Lucas chimed in. "Everyone can tell she likes you. That boy adores you. Don't know why, but it's as clear as day. She was freaking out when she realized her son was missing. But as soon as she got your text she calmed down. She said you had her son, and he was safe. Don't know what's going on in that doomsday head of yours but you need to relax and tell her how you feel. You love her."

"I do not." His defenses shot up without thought. He took a deep breath. The truth was he did love her and that's what scared him the most. For good reason.

"Laying my emotions on her wouldn't be fair. A family is not in my future, and they deserve more than anything I can offer."

Cyrus sighed, as if having to repeat himself to a stubborn child. "She might be leaving the ranch for good unless you say something to her. They were both happy here. I think they need us as much as you need them. You have to stop running and let God heal you."

"This doesn't have anything to do with God," Joaquin argued.

"No, it has to do with you being afraid of the gifts God has for you. Afraid of letting yourself be happy because you might lose it all."

His jaw hurt from clenching it so tightly. Shadow laid his paws on Joaquin's thighs and licked under his chin. He hugged the dog close. "That's not an unrealistic fear. You know that better than anyone."

Cyrus nodded. "Do I wish things had turned out different? That our parents were here tonight celebrating with us? That Tita was cooking? Yes. Do I miss Charlene every day, and does it hurt to watch our daughter grow up without her? Yes. But it's the memories and love we shared that stay with us. If we hadn't had them in our lives, we wouldn't have experienced the joy of loving them and each other. You and Lali could have all of that happiness. Are you willing to let her and Oscar and you miss out on that possibility?"

In the cold darkness, the sleet grew heavier as the wind whispered to the trees and the clear water kept flowing. But the brothers sat still with him.

"What about you, Lucas? Any words of wisdom on how I'm messing up everyone's life?"

With his feet still in the frigid water, Lucas leaned forward and braced his arms on the edge of the rock. After a bit he looked up and the humor was gone. "I'll leave the wisdom to Cyrus. But I do have to point out you've been more like the brother I remember from my childhood since our cave expert and her son showed up. Plopped right on your doorstep so you couldn't avoid them."

A long stretch of silence followed those words. Joaquin didn't want to accept the truth in them. "That kid is gone forever."

Cyrus nodded. "Traumatic events change us. But at the core we're the same. We've seen glimpses of the old Joaquin since Lali and Oscar's arrival. Why are you afraid of him resurfacing?"

Joaquin's throat tightened, leaving him unable to form words. He planted his elbows on his knees and leaned his forehead into his palms.

Cyrus dropped his strong hand on Joaquin's shoulder. "I want my brother back, the one who would walk up to Lali and tell her how he feels without fear holding him back. What if she loves you? What if you're exactly what she and Oscar need to have the best life possible? God has given you an opportunity to find joy and bring joy to others. You'd be selfish to run. Can you really live without them?"

His heart slammed against his chest. "Have they already left?"

Cyrus checked his watch. "Probably."

Lucas was putting his socks and boots back on. "If you go straight across the Tres Amigos front pasture you should be able to cut them off on the highway. Go get your girl."

Joaquin stood. An army of fire ants swarmed his gut. "Is this the right thing to do? Run after her and stop her from leaving?"

"You're just going to tell her how you feel. Let

her decide if she stays or not. Either way, we'll be at the house. If you need us, we're here."

Not allowing his brain to take him in circles, he charged up the slope, slipping a couple of times. Ice was already forming on the rocks. She shouldn't be driving in this. He mounted Maverick and charged through the line of trees into the pasture. Shadow barked with excitement.

With the path clear of rocks and trees, he leaned forward and urged the horse to run. The hard pounding of hooves on the grassland was the only sound as they moved as one to the highway.

The gates were too far. They would have to go over the fence. As they got closer, he leaned against Maverick's neck and readied for the jump. Once they landed, he sat up and Maverick came to a sliding stop.

On the edge of the paved road, he looked both ways. No cars. He was too late.

He pulled out his phone. Should he call her? Where was she going tonight? Why had he avoided her instead of asking about her plans?

Now that he was out of his end-of-the-world headspace it was clear he'd rather be with her than hiding in the mountains of Mexico. They could build a life together, on the ranch, if she wanted him in her life as much as he wanted her.

He could hear the sleet hitting against the road. It was getting dangerous to be out in this weather. Headlights popped over the hill from his ranch.

Yes! He waved the vehicle down, the ridiculous grin needing to be tempered back.

The black SUV slowed and pulled onto the narrow shoulder. It wasn't hers. He rode up and waited for the window to roll down. Her father was driving. Was she with them?

It hadn't occurred to him that he'd have to do this in front of her parents and ex.

"Joaquin? Que esta sucediendo?" The older man's usual stoic expression was in a full frown as he asked what was happening.

Joaquin glanced over the older man's should but didn't see Lali or Oscar. Just Matias, alone. Had she stayed behind? "Where's Lali?"

Her ex-fiancé leaned forward. "Sorry, cowboy. She was in such a hurry to leave she didn't wait for us." He gave him a two-finger salute and sat back.

Her mother kept looking forward. "She has unfinished business. Once we get her home, she'll understand her duty."

He wanted to argue with them, but a cold gust of wind hit him, and he pulled his hat down. "The storm's coming in faster and harder than forecasted. You might want to stay at the ranch a little longer."

"No. We have reservations," her father insisted.

"Okay." He backed his horse up. "Y'all travel safe."

The window went up and they were back on the road. Shadow barked. "Nothing left to do, boy."

The wind blew as if telling him to hurry along. *Unfinished business.* Was it the cave or him?

They had to walk into the wind. It was almost as miserable as the pain in his heart. "Sorry, Maverick. You get extra alfalfa tonight." He wanted to sprint back to the ranch but there was no way in this storm. He had been a fool all the way around tonight and his poor horse and dog were suffering.

Shadow barked. A bark was returned. That sounded like... He turned in the saddle. "Luna!" What was she doing out here?

Her barking was urgent. She stopped in the middle of the road and continued to bark at them. Joaquin turned Maverick around to face the Akita. Luna watched him for a heartbeat then spun and ran back toward town.

He frowned as he followed. With one bark Shadow followed Luna into the dark winter night. Dread and fear were mangled in his gut.

How had Luna ended up out here alone?

Whatever was going on, that was Luna's urgent warning bark. Something was wrong.

He nudged Maverick to move faster. "I know, boy. You're the best."

Ahead he saw Luna and Shadow. They were waiting for him on the Williamson Bridge. Bridges were not good. They were the first thing to ice over and it was hard to see in this sleet.

Luna took off across the bridge once he was close. Shadow followed. He wished he had one of Lali's helmets with the light on the front. There. The bridge railing was damaged. He looked down and froze. Below him was Lali's Range Rover, upside down in the shallow river. She must have been driving back to the ranch. A tree had stopped it from being fully submerged, but the driver's side was pinned against the giant cypress. Broken branches had the other doors blocked.

A car accident, just like his parents. He fought the urge to be sick. Lali and Oscar needed him alert and clearheaded. He dismounted and ran down the slope. He had his phone out calling 911, then his brothers.

Please God. Don't let me be too late.

"Momma. Wake up." Oscar's voice in a tunnel. Why was he so far away?

She groaned. Her eyes wouldn't open. Why was it so cold? And what was with all the pounding? Who was pounding on her window?

"Lali! Wake up. Oscar, are you okay?"

Was that Joaquin? "Shut the door," she tried to

say, but the words didn't sound right. The wind was so cold. She tried to pull her blanket around her, but it wouldn't budge. Or was it her? Her arms wouldn't move.

"Joaquin? Oscar?" She tried to answer but her mouth wasn't working either. Her heart crashed into her chest bone. Everything hurt. What was wrong? Breathe. She needed to breathe to figure out what was going on.

Luna was licking her in the face. She wrinkled her nose.

"Momma won't wake up. I told Luna to get you." Oscar sounded scared. She tried to pet Luna, but her arms wouldn't move.

"She's a good dog. I called for help. It's going to be okay." Joaquin sounded close.

"Lali, can you hear me? Oscar is safe. I'm going to get him out then I'll come for you. All the side doors are jammed or obstructed. I'm coming in through the tailgate." As he talked, she heard other muffled sounds and wind. Why was the wind in her room? Pain shot through her head when she attempted to turn around.

Tailgate? It came back to her. She had lost control of the Rover on the bridge.

"Lali? Baby, look at me." Joaquin sounded scared. This must be taking him back to his parents, to the boys in the Middle East. He—

"Lali. Open your eyes." His large hand cupped

her neck, and his fingers gently dug into her skull. His thumb caressed her cheek.

She took a deep breath and focused on lifting her lids. She blinked until his beautiful face came into focus. He was crying. She tried to lift her hand to wipe the silent tears from his face.

"Hey there." He pressed his forehead against hers. "Oscar's safe. He's so smart. Your boy sent Luna to come get me when you wouldn't wake up."

"Thank you." She finally managed to form words. "I can't move my arms." She would not cry.

"You're pinned in." He covered her with his coat then used a towel to wipe her face. "Can you wiggle your fingers and toes?"

She could. "You came for us." He had climbed in from the back and now leaned forward, wedged between her and what was left of the passenger seat.

"I'll always come when you need me, no matter where you are. I love you."

She blinked. Had she heard him correctly?

He lowered his head. "Sorry. This is not the time or place." When he raised his chin, their gazes locked. "I've never been accused of being romantic, but this is bad timing even for me. I just... When I saw the car..." His throat bobbed with the unsaid thought.

The desire to hug him was too much, and she couldn't move her useless arms. If ever a man needed a hug, it was Joaquin in this moment. "I should have called instead of rushing back to the ranch. I've made so many bad decisions. But before the night was over, I had to tell you something, even if you weren't ready to hear it."

He pressed his lips together and searched her eyes.

"I love you," she whispered. "I don't know how the details will play out, but I think we are meant to share a future."

His steel gaze softened. "That might be a concussion talking."

She smiled. "I've allowed other people to tell me who I was. But God brought me here to you and the ranch. He gave me the opportunity to start on the right path. I was coming back to tell you. I love you."

He cupped her face and stared into her eyes. "Yep. Unquestionably concussed." He grinned then looked away from her. "My brothers are here. They have Oscar and the dogs warm in Cyrus's truck. They should be able to pull you out. The ambulance is on the way too. Hold tight. You're going to be okay."

"I'm going to be better than okay."

Chapter Eighteen

Lali pulled the thick blanket tighter around her and snuggled deeper into the corner of the sofa. It had been late afternoon on Christmas Day before the hospital released her. Lucas had spent enough time in Colorado and Montana that he'd had ice gear for his truck for the trip to get her.

Joaquin hadn't been alone with her at the hospital. Her parents had also stayed at her bedside and returned with her to the main house. Matias had stayed at the hotel, saying he had had enough of the DeLeon family and the ranch.

Warmth seeped through Lali. She would never get enough of Joaquin and his family. The ranch felt like home. Despite the broken clavicle and concussion, today felt as if it was the first day of a new, exciting life.

"Mija, is there anything I can get you?" her father asked for the tenth time or so. Her parents sat in cushioned rocking chairs that had been built by Joaquin's great-grandfather. The kitchen was bustling with the traditional Christmas breakfast they had put on hold for her and Oscar's return.

Guilt plagued Lali's parents no matter what she said. The idea they had driven over the bridge that Oscar and she had been trapped under horrified them. "The conditions worsened so fast," her father said. "I wasn't paying attention to anything other than the road."

Her mother laid a reassuring hand on his arm. "You weren't in the car alone. None of us..." Her mother pressed her lips together.

"Oscar and I are fine," she reminded them. "We are all here and safe. It's time to celebrate the gifts God's given us." Being a single mother with parents who didn't understand her son had always weighed on her. What would happen to Oscar if something happened to her?

Now she had no doubts that Joaquin DeLeon and his family would step in and take great care of him. She looked to the kitchen where Abigail and Rigo prepared the late breakfast. They understood how to take care of those who were lost and hurt better than anyone she knew.

Her mother looked down at her hands and smiled. "I always thought it was strange for people to buy their pets a Christmas gift, but Luna deserves a big gift from us."

The accident had proven that a silver lining could be found in every situation. The fear that they could have lost their daughter and grandson has caused her parents to reevaluate their opinions on her staying here and Luna's importance to their lives.

"Mom! Mom!" Oscar burst into the room from the kitchen. "Joaquin says I'm a real cowboy now."

Luna was right next to him, followed by Leo and Joaquin. "The stock tank had frozen over again. Tio Joaquin and Cyrus had to chop it with axes. Oscar and I threw the chunks as far as we could."

"It was so much fun. Then we checked the pump house and the chickens." Oscar's face was red from the cold and excitement. "He said we deserve a hearty breakfast for our hard work."

Her mother teared up again. "You deserve so much more. You're so brave and strong." She turned to Lali. "I can't believe the difference in him." She reached over and put a hand on Lali's arm. "You're a good mother. And I'm so sorry—"

"Mom. It's okay. Thank you."

"You are a good mom." Joaquin's hair was tousled, and his cheeks were a bit red too. He sat next to her and took her hand in his. It was warm; so was his smile. "They were a great help." His voice was low and soothing. "How are you feeling?"

"I don't think I've ever been better."

He raised his brows and scanned her face, probably noting each bruise.

Leo looked at their clasped hands. "Are y'all boyfriend and girlfriend now?"

"Of course they are," Emma said. "He ran his horse across two ranches, jumped fences and swam the Frio in an ice storm to rescue her." The teen gave them a cheeky grin. "Any announcements that need to be made?"

Abigail came up behind her. "Yes. Breakfast is ready." She winked at Lali. "Welcome to the family."

The love and acceptance surrounded her. She was in the right place and was giving her heart and faith to the right man this time.

She couldn't help but smile even bigger when she looked up and found Joaquin staring back at her. "Are you sure you're okay?" he asked. "We can turn off the lights or go to your cabin where it's quieter."

"This is perfect."

He grinned. "I don't know about that, but I might love you even more for saying it."

After everyone finished eating, Rigo stood. "Last night we didn't get to finish the tradition of our favorite songs and story."

Leo clapped. "Read the story, Tito. Tio Joaquin, do you have your guitar?"

"I sure do."

As he moved to get it, Cyrus paused and put an arm around Joaquin's neck. "Welcome home, brother. It's good to have you back."

The two men tightened their hold for a second then separated. There was a dampness in Joaquin's eyes, but Lali didn't think it wise to point that out.

He kept his head down as he tuned his guitar. But his voice was strong as he started them on "O Come, All Ye Faithful" and they finished with the most beautiful rendition of "Silent Night." "Sleep in heavenly peace" settled deep into her heart.

When the singing was done, Tito read a beautiful story of angels announcing the birth of Christ. He told of the shepherds' faithfulness and the journey the wise men made to honor the baby with gifts.

He closed the book. "We show our love to each other by sharing the gifts we have. We did that last night. But I hear there is one gift that still needs to be given." He looked at Joaquin. "Ready?"

Joaquin gently sat his guitar to the side and sat on the floor in front of Oscar. On one knee, he pulled a red box from under the rocker he had been sitting on.

"Oscar, I have a gift for you." He handed the box to her son.

He opened it and lifted out the hand-embroidered dog jacket. Oscar's eyes went wide. Luna sat up and barked. Oscar stood, clenching the custom-made jacket with one hand as he threw himself at Joaquin.

Luna's tail was wagging her whole body. "This is a gift that has strings attached and a contract to sign."

Oscar stepped back as he glanced at Luna then back to Joaquin.

"In this folder—" Joaquin opened it and lifted a paper "—there's a contract that states you promise to love Luna and take care of her every day. Her good days and her bad days."

Lali wiped at her eyes.

"I will always take care of her," her son said with much seriousness. "Always. I promise. The way she took care of me and Momma when we were trapped in the car."

Lali pressed her lips tightly together, hoping to keep from a full-blown sob.

Joaquin pointed to a dog's paw print on the bottom of the paper. "Exactly. She's vowed to always be there for you as a friend and companion. Do you accept this gift?"

He nodded vigorously as Luna's tail wagged. "I do," he whispered.

"Then go ahead and give the first command as her official partner."

Oscar made eye contact with Luna, then signed for her to sit on his right side. Full of joy, the dog did exactly as she was told. Oscar buried his face in her fur.

Joaquin gently slid in next to Lali. He leaned

close to her ear. "I kind of have a gift for you too. But you'll have to be the one to put it together."

Her forehead wrinkled in confusion.

"I got everyone to agree that you can have a team. Come the new year, we trust you to bring in the people you see fit."

"Really?" He trusted her with his heart and his land.

He nodded, his grin saying that he knew he'd done good.

She cupped his face. "But I didn't get you anything."

"That's not true. Every wish I'd been afraid of wanting is right in front of me."

Then she laid her hand over his heart. "I thought the cave was my Christmas gift from God. The ranch was a place to hide while I found the courage to create my own life separate from my parents' aspirations and expectations. But I found so much more. The biggest surprise was the lone cowboy hiding on the hillside with his dogs. You're the gift I will never ever return."

"Merry Christmas, love," he whispered.

"Merry Christmas." She laid her head on his shoulder. Growing up, she had wished for a cozy Christmas full of family and love. Now with Joaquin she had it all.

Epilogue

Valentine's Day

Joaquin rubbed the ring between his finger and thumb. He'd carried it with him since his grandfather had given it to him. The desire to give it to Lali on Christmas Day had been so strong. But he hadn't wanted to scare her by moving too fast.

Each day he spent with her he loved her more. His therapy sessions had moved from his PTSD to his fear of losing the people he loved. And his fear of telling them he loved them, as though that was the reason he'd lost them.

In that fear he had been pushing them away and losing all the opportunity to love them or be loved by them. Ironic.

"What has you smiling?" Lali asked as they walked up the steps to the main house. Earlier he had taken advantage of the beautiful mild weather to take Lali and Oscar on horseback to his favorite spot by the river. He had surprised them with a picnic. Oscar had wanted to jump in the river, but he'd have to wait for warmer weather. He had almost asked her there. But once again, it hadn't felt right.

Now he knew why.

Leo met them at the door and immediately took Oscar and Luna out the back. He'd released Shadow so he could play with them.

Before any of his family could interrupt, he pulled her up the steps. "Come here. There something I want to show you."

She followed him up the stairs. They passed the wall of photos taken of all the generations that had worked on this land and left behind a legacy of love. Oscar and Lali were going to be a part of this legacy.

At the top he stopped. They stood in silence for a moment, studying the nine-by-twelve photo. She touched the edge of the frame and waited for him.

He took a moment to look at each person in the picture, the joy and love that had saturated that day. "This was taken a month after they brought the twins home. It was a good day." His voice sounded rough to his own ears. In the photo his grandmother held Isaac and his father proudly cradled his infant daughter, Abigail. His mother had one arm around an eight-year-old smiling Lucas and Cyrus stood behind their grandfather.

"So, you were like twelve in this picture. You're already taller than Cyrus. Rigo looks so young. You all do."

"I stopped coming upstairs after we lost them. I haven't looked at this photo in years. All I saw was everything we'd lost. They should have been celebrating with us at all the milestones. I was angry for so long. Then the sadness of their absence overshadowed any joy I should have found. This picture made me face all the ugly feelings, so I avoided it. I avoided my family."

She turned to him. "Now what do you see?"

His gaze went from the portrait to her. "The legacy they worked so hard to build. Love. Joy. My parents would be so proud of my siblings."

"They'd be proud of you too."

He snorted. "It's been a long road. But I know they would love you and Oscar." He looked at the portrait again and smiled. "They would be very proud of where I'm at right now."

His heart rate picked up at the thought of this incredible woman wanting to be near him. He took her hand and sat on the top step. She joined him. Her head tilted with an unspoken question as she held his gaze.

"There was something I wanted to give you at Christmas, but I was afraid it was too soon. Then… Well." He glanced at the portrait. "I don't want to spend another day in fear. Or putting off the opportunity to love you completely and selfishly to be loved by you."

He took the gold ring out of his pocket. "Tito gave this to me on the day my baby sister got married." He lifted it to her in offering. "Dr. Xitlali Kan, would you do me the honor of being my wife and building a family with me? I love you so much."

Sweat beaded on his forehead as she blinked at the ring. It had been too fast. "We can go to Mexico together. Study caves wherever you want. You're my home. I—"

She wrapped her hand around his. "You're in every beat of my heart. You're proof that dreams and wishes come true. Even the ones I was afraid to ask for. God knew my heart. He brought me home to you."

"Is that a yes?"

She laughed, then cupped his face and kissed him. "Yes, Joaquin DeLeon. I will be your wife."

With her in his arms he was no longer afraid to march into the future with love. God's gifts were great indeed and he would never take them for granted.

*****

If you liked this story from Jolene Navarro, check out her previous Love Inspired books:

**The Texan's Unexpected Home
The Texan's Journey Home
The Reluctant Rancher**

Available now from Love Inspired!

*Find more great reads at
www.LoveInspired.com.*

Dear Reader,

The verse at the beginning of the book reflects so much on the content of this story. Obviously, it's about Christmas, but also the shepherds who stayed alert over the night to protect the ones they were responsible for. Waiting in faith to hear the word of God. Joaquin has the heart of a shepherd. Not for just his family and the people who enter his domain, but for the land and its history.

My inspiration for the DeLeon family came from a visit to the Briscoe Western Art Museum. If you find yourself on the River Walk in San Antonio, make sure to visit. I discovered the extensive collection belonging to the Guerra Family of South Texas, whose legacy spans over 400 years in what we now know as Texas. This family has been instrumental in collecting and preserving Texas's ranching history and culture.

Being a seventh-generation Texan, I grew up with stories about the six flags that have flown over Texas; the Guerra family has experienced all of them. I aimed to create a family in the Texas Hill Country imbued with a similar legacy tied to the land, rich with history.

I hope you enjoy reading stories about my fictional town of Rio Bella, and the DeLeon family. Abigail and Kingston's story can be found in *The Texan's Unexpected Home*. The next story belongs to Isaac DeLeon.

Blessings,
Jolene

Get up to 4 Free Books!

We'll send you 2 free books from each series you try PLUS a free Mystery Gift.

FREE Value Over **$25**

Both the **Love Inspired®** and **Love Inspired® Suspense** series feature compelling novels filled with inspirational romance, faith, forgiveness and hope.

YES! Please send me 2 FREE novels from the Love Inspired or Love Inspired Suspense series and my FREE gift (gift is worth about $10 retail). After receiving them, if I don't wish to receive any more books, I can return the shipping statement marked "cancel." If I don't cancel, I will receive 6 brand-new Love Inspired Larger-Print books or Love Inspired Suspense Larger-Print books every month and be billed just $7.19 each in the U.S. or $7.99 each in Canada. That is a savings of 20% off the cover price. It's quite a bargain! Shipping and handling is just 50¢ per book in the U.S. and $1.25 per book in Canada.* I understand that accepting the 2 free books and gift places me under no obligation to buy anything. I can always return a shipment and cancel at any time by calling the number below. The free books and gift are mine to keep no matter what I decide.

Choose one:
- ☐ **Love Inspired Larger-Print** (122/322 BPA G36Y)
- ☐ **Love Inspired Suspense Larger-Print** (107/307 BPA G36Y)
- ☐ **Or Try Both!** (122/322 & 107/307 BPA G36Z)

Name (please print)

Address   Apt. #

City   State/Province   Zip/Postal Code

Email: Please check this box ☐ if you would like to receive newsletters and promotional emails from Harlequin Enterprises ULC and its affiliates. You can unsubscribe anytime.

Mail to the Harlequin Reader Service:
IN U.S.A.: P.O. Box 1341, Buffalo, NY 14240-8531
IN CANADA: P.O. Box 603, Fort Erie, Ontario L2A 5X3

Want to explore our other series or interested in ebooks? Visit www.ReaderService.com or call 1-800-873-8635.

---

*Terms and prices subject to change without notice. Prices do not include sales taxes, which will be charged (if applicable) based on your state or country of residence. Canadian residents will be charged applicable taxes. Offer not valid in Quebec. This offer is limited to one order per household. Books received may not be as shown. Not valid for current subscribers to the Love Inspired or Love Inspired Suspense series. All orders subject to approval. Credit or debit balances in a customer's account(s) may be offset by any other outstanding balance owed by or to the customer. Please allow 4 to 6 weeks for delivery. Offer available while quantities last.

Your Privacy—Your information is being collected by Harlequin Enterprises ULC, operating as Harlequin Reader Service. For a complete summary of the information we collect, how we use this information and to whom it is disclosed, please visit our privacy notice located at https://corporate.harlequin.com/privacy-notice. Notice to California Residents – Under California law, you have specific rights to control and access your data. For more information on these rights and how to exercise them, visit https://corporate.harlequin.com/california-privacy. For additional information for residents of other U.S. states that provide their residents with certain rights with respect to personal data, visit https://corporate.harlequin.com/other-state-residents-privacy-rights/.

LIRLIS25